KILLING IN CARTUNA

Travelling home from a wedding, El Paso detective Cord Wheeler stops at the New Mexico town of Cartuna. Walking to his hotel he hears a woman scream and then he's slugged from behind. The woman has been murdered, the third killing in recent months. Wheeler agrees to help the sheriff by taking a job guarding a cattle drive in order to trap the criminals. Will he discover the real reason behind the killings and bring the guilty to justice?

GEORGE J. PRESCOTT

KILLING IN CARTUNA

Complete and Unabridged

LINFORD
Leicester

First published in Great Britain in 2006 by
Robert Hale Limited
London

First Linford Edition
published 2008
by arrangement with
Robert Hale Limited
London

British Library CIP Data

Prescott, George J.
  Killing in Cartuna.—Large print ed.—
Linford western library
1. Western stories
2. Large type books
I. Title
823.9′2 [F]

ISBN 978–1–84782–131–7

Published by
F. A. Thorpe (Publishing)
Anstey, Leicestershire

Set by Words & Graphics Ltd.
Anstey, Leicestershire
Printed and bound in Great Britain by
T. J. International Ltd., Padstow, Cornwall

1

It was the morning sun slanting through the barred window of his cell that woke Cord Wheeler. Reluctantly, he swung his legs off the roughly made bunk and tried unsuccessfully to rub the sleep from his eyes, before gingerly feeling at the egg-sized lump decorating the back of his head.

More or less awake, he was searching his rumpled clothes for the inevitable black cigar, when a not unfriendly voice said, 'That bed ain't perzactly the most comfortable you've ever slept on, I'm bettin'.'

Wheeler paused in his search and looked up to find himself being examined by a pair of faded blue eyes in a seamed, smiling face burnt to the colour of an old saddle by the New Mexican sun and wind.

Easing himself back on the bunk

1

without replying, Wheeler's surreptitious scrutiny took in the twinkle behind the blue eyes, before moving on to the scuffed belt with the worn-butted Colts in their battered, greasy holsters.

'You ain't wrong . . . Marshal?' Wheeler replied questioningly, and the old man nodded, the easy grin spreading across his face as he hooked back his greasy leather vest to display the six-pointed star.

'You called it about right,' he admitted, advancing carefully into the narrow space that allowed access to the cells.

'Name's Bregan, Al Bregan,' he went on, settling himself comfortably against the wall opposite the door of Wheeler's cell. 'My deputy ain't much use for anything else but he makes a good cup o' coffee. Feel like one?'

'What I'd really like, Marshal,' Wheeler snarled, 'is for you and that misbegotten son of a whore who got sportin' that badge to get off your goddam fat asses and find the son of a bitch who murdered that girl!'

'I figger mebbe we got him right here,' came the soft reply, 'but I'm willing to be convinced otherwise.'

'Now, suppose we have that coffee,' Bregan went on, 'and you tell me your side of it . . . ?'

★   ★   ★

The coffee went some way to restoring Wheeler's good temper and with a cigar going to his satisfaction, he shrugged and said. 'To be honest, Marshal, there ain't that much to tell.' He paused, ordering his thoughts. 'I'd been down south, to try and stop a young feller who's a good friend o' mine from gettin' hisself into trouble,' he began whimsically, before adding quickly, as the peace officer's face hardened, 'Oh, it weren't nothin' like that, Marshal. The boy was figgerin' on gettin' hisself hitched. Miz Delia is a sure 'nough top-dollar gal, but me and Sly felt it our solemn duty to try and talk young

Hooper out of it an' when we couldn't, weren't nothin' to be done but get drunk at the weddin'.'

Wheeler felt it unnecessary to add that, as was his habit, he had celebrated the event with innumerable cups of strong coffee.

'Anyhow,' the man from El Paso resumed, 'we saw the kids off on the train to New Orleans, Miz Delia figgerin' on havin' a bang-up honeymoon before she settled down to bein' a sheriff's wife . . .

'Your compadre's the sheriff of this place you was visitin'?' Bregan interrupted.

'Oh sure,' Wheeler replied innocently. 'They had some trouble down there, a rustlin' gang and such, coupla months ago and I helped the boys clean house. After the dust settled they elected young Hooper county sheriff, on account of the old one, who was part o' the rustlin' gang, being suddenly taken dead, then, damn it, he goes and . . . '

'Whoa there, son,' Bregan pushed in

4

again. 'How was it you was cleanin' up a rustlin' gang?'

'Oh, didn't I say' Wheeler responded mildly. 'That was because up in El Paso I'm what you might call a private detective.'

'A detective!' Bregan snapped, staring hard at the slim hard-looking individual, with the cold green eyes, who was occupying the largest of the jail's two cells.

'So what about last night?' he demanded abruptly, dragging his furiously racing thoughts back to the present.

'I'd just hit town,' Wheeler began, 'Cartuna being the night stopover for the through stage to El Paso. I'd had what passes for dinner in that hole on Main Street that calls itself a saloon and I was heading back to the stage depot when I heard a scream. Sounded like it come from an alley up the street a little ways, so I headed up there.'

'And?' Bregan prompted.

'Well.' Wheeler shrugged. 'You can

bet your life I weren't runnin' into no alley without checkin' who might be waitin' there, so I knelt down and looked round the corner. Got a look at what must have been the killer runnin' away, but all I saw was his back in the moonlight.'

'Wouldn't recognize him again, I suppose?' Bregan asked, although plainly without much hope.

'Sorry, Marshal.' Wheeler shrugged. 'He was dressed like a cowboy is about all I can tell you and I'm guessin' cowpunchers ain't exactly uncommon hereabouts.'

'Only about as thick as fleas on an ol' dog,' Bregan growled morosely.

'Anyhow,' Wheeler went on, 'I slipped up the side of the alley out o' the moonlight, in case this feller had company and found the woman lyin' where he left her. I was checkin' to see if she was alive when some son of a bitch whomped me on the back of the head.'

'Next thing I know,' Wheeler finished,

settling back and drawing on his foul-smelling cigar, 'I woke up here with a lump like a hen's egg on the back o' my skull and what feels like an almighty hangover.'

Before Bregan could reply the door connecting the cells to the front office was pushed unceremoniously open and a squat Apache shouldered his silent, muscular way through it.

Wheeler had just time to take in the long grey hair and flat, intelligent face with its brown button eyes, before Bregan was taking his hand away from the Colt to which reflex had sent it and demanding in guttural Apache, 'Well what did you find, mule-eater? Is the white-eye lyin?'

'You don't pay me enough to insult me, Al,' the Indian began in surprisingly good English. 'And your 'white-eye' speaks Apache, unless I miss my guess,' he went on, having caught Wheelers' fleeting grin.

''Mule-eater' ain't very nice, Marshal,' Wheeler chided in confirmation.

'Especially between blood brothers.'

'You got quick eyes, Mr Wheeler,' Bregan snapped irritably. 'This here is Joe Ironhand. He's my brother in blood and been my side partner for more years than either of us can remember. So what did you find?' Bregan repeated, glaring at the Indian.

'Don't know yet.' Ironhand shrugged.

'Lift your foot,' he went on, addressing Wheeler.

'Not him,' Ironhand stated simply, after a minute study of the sole of Wheeler's boot. 'Though he was there. Moved up the side of the alley and then stepped across to the girl. Other man did the killing, though,' the Apache finished.

'How did it look?' Bregan asked, sighing disgustedly. 'Same as before?'

'Sure,' the other agreed. 'Left tracks this time. Big man, long stride, big boots, could have been any of a dozen you see around town every day.'

'Did you recognize the tracks?' Wheeler asked mildly.

8

'Nope,' Ironhand admitted. 'He was smart, knew enough to disguise his walk and he was runnin' when he left.'

'Anyhow, this ain't gettin' us nowhere,' Bregan snapped, reaching down to produce the key to the cell, which he unlocked.

'If this worthless renegade says it weren't you, that's good enough . . . '

'Dallas says to come get dinner now, Al,' Ironhand interrupted. 'And I ain't gonna be the one to make her mad. Besides,' he went on with a grin, 'If you ain't there, I'll eat your share too.'

'Goddamn it . . . ' Bregan began, then subsided, plainly lost for words. 'Come and eat with us, Mr Wheeler,' he offered abruptly. 'My daughter's the best cook in town.'

'Sure,' Wheeler smilingly replied, following Bregan out of the cells area and accepting his cane and the ivory-butted Smith and Wesson from the old Apache. 'But 'Mr Wheeler' sure makes me feel old,' he went on. 'My friends call me Cord and I'm sure hopin' I can include both of you in that.'

★ ★ ★

A short walk brought the three men to Bregan's house, a neat adobe on the outskirts of town. The door was opened by a slim, demure-looking young Apache woman.

'This here is my daughter, Cord,' Bregan began abruptly. 'And just so you ain't mistook about nothin', Joe Ironhand ain't just my brother in blood, he's my brother-in-law, too.'

'Got a boy, too,' Bregan went on quickly, 'but Travis is out helping Doc Gilmore. He's aimin' to go to medical school as soon as we can scratch up the necessary.'

'Miz Bregan,' Wheeler began, removing his hat and bending over the young woman's hand, with just the right touch of New Orleans courtliness. 'It's sure my pleasure to make your acquaintance, ma'am.'

'Why, thank you, sir, and I'd be obliged if you'd call me Dallas,' the girl responded, bobbing a curtsy. 'And if you track dirt in on my clean floor that I just mopped, Uncle Joe,' she went on waspishly, 'guess who's gonna be cleanin' it up! Wipe your feet and you too, Pa, then bring Mr Wheeler through to the kitchen.'

'Just like her ma,' Bregan assured Wheeler softly, as the girl glided out of sight.

'Sure,' Joe Ironhand grunted. 'Just like her ma. You never beat her enough, either.'

'Now, Joe, you know why I never laid a hand on Deer That Walks . . . ' Bregan began reasonably.

'Sure,' the old Apache growled, although his wide grin belied the sting in his words, 'It's because she was tougher than you. Hell, she was tougher than me,' he finished.

'And better with a Bowie knife,' Bregan added slyly.

★　★　★

'I'm sayin' plain that I can't get a line on this whole business, Cord,' Bregan admitted, leaning back and pulling on a good cigar. 'An' it's sure losin' me sleep.'

Having done full justice to his daughter's excellent dinner, Bregan and his guest had taken their coffee out on to the wide, shady veranda that ran across the back of the house.

Settled in comfortable chairs and joined by Joe Ironhand, clutching his after-dinner glass of whiskey, Bregan seemed at a loss after his initial statement.

'I'm takin' it that this ain't the first killin' you've had around here?' Wheeler asked mildly.

'Third,' Ironhand grunted, when Bregan said nothing.

'And the other two,' Wheeler asked, 'did they happen just like this one?'

'We figure so,' Bregan answered, with a scowl at his partner. 'Only we was careless with the first one, on account of it was just a whore. With the next one, Krantz, the nester's daughter we . . . '

'Hold on, Marshal,' Wheeler interrupted mildly. 'Mebbe you'd better tell it from the beginning.'

'Gal name of Millie Graham was the first,' Bregan began. 'I got word from the marshal of Benbow that she was comin', apparently he'd moved her outta town when she'd been caught with some dude's wallet.'

'She was a pretty l'il thing,' Bregan went on, ignoring Ironhand's cynical grunt. 'But I guess she weren't no better than she should ha' been.'

'Anyhow,' the old man went on, 'she give me some hard-luck story about the wallet bein' a put-up job and asked if she could stay. Whores ain't that common around here and what with the boys from Faulkner's Flying F and a coupla smaller ranches, well, I figured another one couldn't hurt.'

'Sounds like good sense,' Wheeler offered. Bregan nodded his agreement.

'Well, she set up shop above the

saloon with the other gals,' he went on, 'and she had no trouble at all until one night, about three months ago, she was found strangled behind the livery barn.'

'Whores're liable to end up that way,' Wheeler offered cynically. 'It ain't the safest way to make a living.'

'Sure, I'd agree with you,' Bregan said flatly. 'Except about two months after that, we found another gal, this time down by the creek. She'd been strangled, too.'

'OK,' Wheeler admitted. 'Two murders in a town like this and both girls is too much like a coincidence. Anything else to go on?'

'Sure,' Joe Ironhand interrupted. 'Both gals were blonde and they both had a big hank o' hair ripped from the right side o' their heads!'

2

For a moment, a deathly silence pervaded the little group, to be broken eventually by Wheeler.

'Tell me about this second one,' he demanded softly.

'Name was Sarah Krantz,' Bregan began. 'Ol' Levi Krantz's youngest. Levi's a Swede an' when he gets goin' good, you can't hardly tell where his American finishes an' the other begins.'

'Kids and his wife speak good US, though,' Bregan went on. 'An' Levi's a US citizen; family's regular to church.'

'You mean they're decent people,' Wheeler offered mildly.

'S'pose I do,' Bregan conceded. 'Sarah and Dallas was good friends,' he went on. 'But Dallas told me that Sarah was meetin' someone in secret. She wouldn't tell Dallas who it was, said she couldn't on account of her pa wouldn't understand.'

'You got any idea who it might be, Miz Dallas?' Wheeler enquired mildly, as the girl moved from her place in the doorway and gracefully took the vacant seat near her uncle.

'No, Mr Wheeler . . . Cord,' she blushed, before quickly correcting herself. 'Sarah never told me who.'

'You figger it was mebbe because he was married?' Wheeler asked gently.

'It wasn't that,' the girl returned quickly. 'Sarah was my friend and she was decent,' Dallas went on. 'And she wouldn't have let herself get mixed up in something like that.'

'Besides,' she added inconsequentially, 'we were both going to college next fall. I won a scholarship,' she finished proudly, 'so I don't have to wait like poor Travis.'

★   ★   ★

After the girl had left, Wheeler sat apparently lost in thought for a long moment.

'What about this latest one?' he asked, abruptly jerking out of his reverie.

'Just a stranger.' Bregan shrugged. 'She was middle-aged, from Boston, name on her ticket was Beth Sadler.'

'That was how she signed in at the hotel, too,' Joe Ironhand supplemented. 'Seems like she ate there,' the old Apache went on, 'and then mebbe decided to get some air. Sirus Hinge, the desk clerk, saw her leave about seven and that was the last anyone saw of her until Gus Baily found you near the body.'

'This Gus was the one who whomped me?' Wheeler demanded.

'Nope,' Bregan stated flatly. 'Gus is kinda nervous, rides for the Bar T, but he says he found you unconscious next to the body. Hauled you in here 'cause he couldn't see nothin' else to do.'

'You suspect anyone yourself?' Wheeler asked mildly.

'Wade Dixon, ol' Drew Faulkener's foreman, was seen arguing with Millie

Graham a coupla days before she was murdered,' Bregan began thoughtfully. 'But he had an alibi for what we think was the time o' the murder.'

'Claimed he was playin' cards with a bunch o' drovers passin' through on their way north,' Joe Ironhand supplemented.

'What did they say about it?' Wheeler asked.

'Nothin',' Bregan admitted. 'On account of they'd left town by the time we got around to lookin' for them,' he added before Wheeler could ask the obvious question.

'Story sounds a mite thin if you was to ask me,' Wheeler offered.

'Thought so myself,' Bregan agreed with a short nod. 'But one of Morale's girls said she was serving them drinks all night and when the drovers left, Dixon stayed and spent the rest of the night with her.'

'What did you think about that?' Wheeler asked noncommittally.

'Maria ain't exactly long on brains,'

Joe Ironhand began, 'but she ain't stupid, neither. She could be lyin' and . . .'

'And it sure would give her a hold over this Dixon feller if she was,' Wheeler finished for him.

'About what we thought,' Bregan shrugged.

'Let's go look at the late Miz Sadler,' Wheeler grunted thoughtfully.

* * *

Failing to find the doctor at his house, Bregan led the way to the rear of the spacious general store, where Hank Gilmore, the local doctor, had his surgery.

Gilmore was a brisk little man who Wheeler liked at first sight. He and the two lawmen were plainly old cronies and he certainly seemed as mystified by the murders as they were.

'Strangled, just like the other two. Bruises are real plain. Hank o' hair missin', too,' he finished, a trifle impatiently as Wheeler continued his minute examination of the victim's neck.

'Sure,' Wheeler agreed. 'Bruises are real plain.'

'Put your hand here, will you, Joe?' the detective went on, indicating a position on the victim's neck.

Minutely, Wheeler adjusted the Apache's long fingers before motioning him back and repeating the procedure with his own hand.

'What are you looking for, Cord?' Bregan asked as, at Wheeler's request, the elderly doctor moved up next to the body.

'Just a little idea I got,' Wheeler answered shortly. 'Now, can you see them marks, Doc?' he went on.

'No,' Gilmore confirmed. 'Your hand's covering them.'

'No, it ain't,' Wheeler demurred. 'Look again.'

Carefully, he eased back his fingers.

'My fingers go a good half an inch past them bruises,' he explained. 'Except the thumb mark, which is nearly as long.'

'By God, you're right,' Gilmore snapped. 'Here let me try.'

Wheeler moved to one side, the little doctor taking his place before lightly fitting his fingers against the marks.

'Thumb's almost right but your hands are just a mite too wide, Doc,' Wheeler offered after a careful examination.

'But that's impossible!' Bregan began irritably. 'Joe said from his tracks the killer was over six feet . . . '

'Well over,' the Apache interrupted.

'All right, well over,' Bregan resumed irritably, 'but how can a man well over six feet have hands like a woman?'

'Sure a puzzle, ain't it? And I'll tell you something else,' Wheeler went on mildly. 'That feller I saw runnin' away weren't no bigger'n me. Let's go look at where Miz Sadler was killed.'

* * *

'He left this way, running fast,' Joe Iron-hand explained, indicating the heelless

21

tracks which finished on the rough board-walk behind the saloon.

'No way even an Apache could tell who he was from these,' Wheeler conceded, rising and dusting his hands. 'Are there any more?'

'What's left were all scuffed up when Gus dragged you off to jail,' Bregan admitted. 'Young Gus ain't no lawman and he probably never thought to be careful about tracks.'

'What about whoever slugged me when I was bendin' over Miz Sadler?' Wheeler asked.

'I'm guessin' it musta been the same man,' Joe Ironhand offered. 'And he was real careful,' he went on, leading the way round the disturbed sand and squatting on his heels by another patch, which had plainly been recently swept clean.

'After he slugged you, Cord,' the old Indian began, 'he went back to that doorway, where he'd been hiding, I'm guessin' before he killed the woman, collected a switch from that old mesquite and then wiped his trail clean. Did a good job, too,' Ironhand acknowledged. 'There ain't a mark to be seen, except where he's swept.'

'Like you said,' Wheeler acknowledged, 'careful, real careful. But why go to all that trouble and then not wipe out his other tracks that led out of the alley? And how'd he get round behind me so quick? Did you say this is the first time the killer had left any tracks?'

'That's right,' Bregan answered, Ironhand adding a grunt of agreement. 'Wind'd wiped out the tracks by the time we found Millie and Sarah was killed down by the river and there ain't nothin' but rock down there, so whoever done it didn't leave no marks.'

'Mebbe he sneaked up behind you while you was busy with the body, Cord,' Bregan offered, when Wheeler made no acknowledgement.

'Mebbe,' Wheeler agreed, apparently ignoring Ironhand's grunt of disbelief.

★ ★ ★

Back in the front office of the jail, Bregan gave vent to his frustration.

'I'm tellin' you, Cord, this business has got me beat all which ways. What I can't figger out is why is he's doin' it?'

'He?' Wheeler asked mildly. 'Them marks on Miz Sadler's neck could easy have been made by a woman.'

'Sure,' Bregan bridled impatiently. 'But you don't really think that, do you?'

'Mebbe not,' Wheeler admitted, 'but there are a coupla things about Miz Sadler's murder that don't quite add up.'

'Like?' Bregan demanded impatiently.

'Well first of all, what was a lady, a for real lady like her, doing in an alley behind a saloon? OK, the hotel clerk, this Hinge *hombre*, said she went out for a walk in the early evening but I heard her screams or at least, a scream, about ten o'clock so where was she between the time she left the hotel and the time I found her?' Wheeler demanded.

'I hate to think this, Cord,' Bregan began apprehensively, 'but do you figger we got some sort of mad killer on the loose?

'After all,' the marshal went on anxiously, 'all them gals was blonde and had that hank o' hair missin', kinda like a trophy. I read that they'd caught a killer like that up in Chicago, only he was collectin' the women's reticules.'

'And that's another thing,' Wheeler went on remorselessly, 'where is her reticule?'

'Lady like that don't go nowhere without her bag, case she needs, oh, a handkerchief or scent or such like,' he explained, seeing the look of puzzlement cross the old lawman's face.

'I'm guessin' mebbe Deer That Walks didn't have nothin' like that,' Wheeler grinned. 'So you may be kinda lackin' in that sorta experience.'

Bregan flashed a quick smile at the mild joke but his eyes were looking very inward as he replied, 'Nope, she only ever carried a bag, deer skin, what she made herself. Kept her sewing, one o' Travis' baby teeth, stuff like that, in it.'

'But I can sure tell you, Cord, fancy fixin's or not she was one hell of a good woman. One hell of a woman,' the old lawman repeated absently.

And Wheeler, whose own experience of women had been less than kind, could only smile gently and maintain a thoughtful silence.

★　★　★

Old habits die hard and like the ex-cowhand that he was, Wheeler rolled out of his blankets with the sun and, having breakfasted, set out to look the town of Cartuna over.

He had re-examined the scene of the last killing, without finding anything new and after taking a stroll down to the river to examine the place the Krantz girl had been killed, its location having been minutely described to him by Joe Ironhand, he found himself back on Main Street and outside the saloon, along about first drink time.

'Why'd you want her?' the portly,

middle-aged bartender began, after names had been exchanged and Wheeler had ordered a cigar while inquiring about Millie Graham.

'Friend o' mine, whiskey drummer, was through here a while back, told me if I was down this way and ever wanted myself a good time, she was the gal to look up,' Wheeler explained, grinning sheepishly and leaning awkwardly on the heavy, brass-headed cane.

'Well, she ain't here no more,' the bartender, who'd given his name as Joe Berris, continued. 'On account o' she was murdered!'

'Hell, that sure is tough luck,' Wheeler said incredulously. 'Although a whore's more'n likely to pass out her checks that way, I guess.'

'Marshal got any idea who did it?' he went on guilelessly.

'Well, I heard that he thought it might be Wade Dixon, Faulkener's foreman . . . ' Berris began doubtfully.

'You don't sound so sure yourself, friend?' Wheeler offered mildly.

In answer, the man behind the bar looked carefully to the right and left before saying in a low voice, 'I know it couldn't be ol' Wade on account of he ain't got no use for a whore.'

'How's that?' Wheeler asked innocently. 'I figgered any man'd have a use for a whore sometime?'

'Sure,' Berris returned confidentially, while at the same time dropping his voice, 'but one of the gals told me, ol' Wade, he can't . . . ' and Wheeler, carefully masking his surprise, nodded at the obscene but perfectly explanatory gesture.

3

'You figger he's a cissy man?' Wheeler asked almost conversationally, using the old Cheyenne term with its implied hint of homosexuality, while his mind was poring over the implications of this new-found knowledge.

'Naw, nuthin like that,' Berris muttered, clearly wondering if he had perhaps said too much to this new-found acquaintance.

'Look, mister,' the man behind the bar went on nervously, 'I wouldn't want this to get around, you know. Wade Dixon's a good customer around here and it's only the say so of a two-dollar whore . . . '

'Sure,' Wheeler answered, all genial assurance. 'That whore though, what did you say her name was? She still around?'

'Her name was Velma,' Brevis responded

suspiciously 'And she ain't here no more. What's it to you, anyhow?'

'Why, nothing at all,' came the smiling reply. 'Just thought if that Millie gal weren't here, might be some other lady who'd accommodate a sportin' gentleman.'

*　　*　　*

'Sure,' Bregan began thoughtfully, 'I knew her. Decent gal, never gave no trouble,' he went on, shuffling through a collection of papers in the bottom draw of his desk.

Eventually, with a grunt of satisfaction, the old peace officer eased himself upright, placing a single piece of paper on the ancient, battered desk.

'Full name was Velma Dobbs, said she come from some town back East,' Bregan began. 'Left about five, six months ago. She got beat up pretty bad, but wouldn't say who did it. Took the stage East as soon as she was well enough to travel. Me and Joe figgered some john musta beat her up and that she was too scared to say who it was, 'cause somethin' worse mighta come her way.'

'Sounds likely,' Wheeler admitted thoughtfully.

'Why're you interested, Cord?' Bregan demanded.

'Oh, just fillin' in the pieces,' Wheeler admitted absently, before asking, 'This Velma friends with Millie Graham?'

'Who knows?' Bregan shrugged. 'They was both whores, lived and worked in the same place. I guess they coulda been friends.'

'Friends or not,' Wheeler began, 'they sure musta . . . '

He was interrupted by Joe Ironhand, abruptly pushing through the door. Before either of the two white men could speak, the Indian held up his right hand.

'This what you call a reticule, Cord?' Ironhand demanded softly, indicating the small, dust-smeared velvet bag.

'Sure,' Wheeler admitted, reaching up

to take Ironhand's trophy, 'where'd you find it?'

'Entrance to the alley behind the Wells Fargo depot,' came the swift answer, as Wheeler drew the strings apart, apparently oblivious to Bregan's swiftly indrawn breath and the flickering glance Joe Ironhand threw at his partner.

Apart from a handkerchief, stage ticket in the woman's name and some loose change, the little bag held nothing more, so Wheeler turned his attention to the reticule itself.

Along one side, barely visible except to one who was looking for it, he found a minute tear with several off-white particles adhering to it. For several seconds, Wheeler examined his discovery, even carefully sniffing at the fabric until with a grunt of satisfaction, he placed it carefully to one side and leaning back in his chair, surveyed his two companions.

'OK, what is it about where this was found that's got you two old coots runnin' round like a coupla mother hens lookin' for their only chick?' he demanded.

With a despairing glance at his partner, Bregan admitted, 'Hank Gilmore's got his surgery in that part of town.'

'And you figger that means . . . ?' Wheeler prompted.

'I never told you this yesterday but Travis ain't got an alibi for the nights of any o' them killin's,' the old man began. 'He's been awful edgy lately and I'm just wondering . . . '

'It can't be the boy,' Ironhand threw in. 'He ain't tall enough.'

'Footprints can be faked, Joe,' Bregan answered, misery in every line of his face. 'You know that and so does Travis. God knows you taught him well enough.'

'Now, just hold on a minute, Marshal,' Wheeler offered gently. 'You got anything else to go on apart from suspicions?'

'I saw Dallas washing his shirt this mornin',' Bregan admitted wearily. 'She tried to keep me from seeing, but well, I saw what looked like blood on the sleeve.'

'Workin' for a doctor, he's likely enough to get bloodied up,' Wheeler offered reasonably. 'Anyone else live or got an office down there?'

'Sure,' Joe Ironhand snapped before Bregan could answer, 'Milt Gilmore's got his law office right next door to his daddy's place.'

'He's Hank's only boy,' Bregan began in explanation, as Wheeler settled back and steepled his hands. 'He's some older than Travis and I figger that's why they never really took to each other. His ma, Stella, died birthin' him and . . . well I guess it affected him some way.'

'Sure,' Ironhand grunted. 'It affected him. What Al don't say is that he was bad to start with.'

'Oh sure,' he went on, holding up one hand in the Indian's universal peace sign. 'Ain't none better than old Hank. We both know that an' I ain't arguing.

But that boy's an outlaw clean through. Only one answer to what ails him,' the old Apache finished, 'an' that's a bullet.'

'Anything on him?' Wheeler asked mildly.

'No!' Bregan snapped, giving his old-time friend a white hot glare which affected Joe Ironhand not in the slightest.

'I'm admitting,' Bregan went on more reasonably, turning to Wheeler, 'the boy puts on airs and he sure don't like livin' way out here with us hicks, but last time I looked that weren't a crime.'

'No one's arguing about that,' Ironhand snapped back. 'But you heard them stories that come down from El Paso, after he got back, same as I did.'

'What kinda stories?' Wheeler asked.

'Oh, the usual thing, I guess,' Bregan began reluctantly. 'Gamblin', whores and there was some talk about a coupla gals gettin' hurt at some high-class cathouse.'

'You got a name for the place?' Wheeler asked.

'Leonardo's was what I heard it called,' Bregan stated.

'Listen, Cord,' the old peace officer went on vehemently, 'I hushed them stories up, 'cause Hank Gilmore is about the best human being I know. Every boy needs to sow a few wild oats and I figgered that was all it was. Since he's been back, Milt ain't even been to the saloon as far as I know. Hell, he's courtin' Drew Faulkener's daughter, Maddy.'

'You could be right, o' course,' Wheeler agreed. 'He wouldn't be the first to have settled down after he met the right woman.'

Wheeler saw no reason to reveal to either man that he was aware of the brothel in El Paso called Leonardo's as well as being familiar with the specialized activities its owner, Woo Lee, his employees and their customers indulged in.

★   ★   ★

36

'Them Flying F boys don't exactly look as if they was headin' for a church social, Joe,' Wheeler offered.

'Cord, you just don't know the half of it,' his companion assured him.

The two men were sitting on the scuffed boardwalk which had been built across the front of the jail, watching a group of five riders swinging down in front of the saloon. Four were simple examples of the usual hardcases found all too often in the grass country, while the last of the five was a fresh-faced youngster who seemed out of place in such company. It was this one's pony which had shied sideways, revealing its brand and provoking Wheeler's comment.

'They don't look like they could tell one end of a steer from the other, although I'm bettin' high they know a l'il mite more about six-guns,' Wheeler stated bluntly. 'You have much trouble with them waddies?' he asked.

'There's a couple thought 'cause me and Al ain't as young as we was, that

37

the town needed a l'il hoorawin',' the old man responded, squinting hard across the street as he studied the hitching rail.

'And?' Wheeler asked, raising an eyebrow.

'They thought different after Al beat three of 'em half to death.'

'Where was you?' Wheeler asked with a grin. 'Gittin' too old fer a fight?'

'Listen, white-eye.' The old man grinned back, rising like a cat and moving towards the door of the jail. 'Long as I got a gun and a knife, I ain't dirtyin' my hands on no cowhand.'

'Joe,' Wheeler said softly, causing the old man to pause in the doorway. 'Al ain't thinkin' too clear about young Travis. I wouldn't worry about the boy if'n I was you . . . or him,' he finished meaningly.

Left alone, Wheeler was pondering the case that had been dropped in his lap, when his attention was drawn to a dainty pinto pony, trotting gaily up the dusty Main Street.

Its lady rider was no less eye-catching, long, thick blonde hair, topping a striking face, kept from being simply pretty by a firm chin and the wide, generous mouth.

The girl pulled her mount to a halt in front of the big general store and swung down, just as a slim, dark young man backed through the doorway almost into the girl's arms.

From where Wheeler sat, her smile and flustered look spoke volumes and the man from El Paso was just settling down to enjoy the young man's obvious embarrassment, when three of the Lazy F punchers staggered out of the saloon.

The youngster was in the lead and, catching sight of the girl he lurched towards her, face darkening.

'Get away from that goddamn 'breed, sis,' the boy ordered, coming up next to the pair and grabbing the girl's arm. 'And you, Travis, stay the hell away from my sister!'

'Mind your own business, Charlie,' the girl snapped waspishly, wrenching her arm away. 'When I need your advice, I'll sure let you know.'

'Goddamn it, sis, you can't go round actin' like you want to be some Apache squaw . . .'

'That'll be about enough from you, Charlie!' the dark-haired boy interrupted. 'You ain't so all fired particular about skin colour when you go visitin' your *chiquita*, are you?'

For a moment, the young cowboy stood stock still, his face reddening, then, with a scream of rage, he lunged at his tormentor, throwing a clumsy punch at the other's head.

Only Travis wasn't there. Indian-quick, the dark-haired boy twisted aside, catching the cowboy's forearm and pulling him off balance to land sprawling face down in the dust, half stunned.

It might have ended there, but before the dark boy could move, he felt his arms grabbed from behind and expertly pinned to his side.

'Looks like we gotta hand this here

Indian another lesson, don't it, Breck?' a coarse voice, with a high nasal whine, said in his ear.

'Sure do, Sol, it sure do,' another voice rumbled, as the second of Charlie Faulkener's companions moved round in front of the younger Bregan.

'If you want to keep ridin' for my father, you just let Travis go, Breck Barker!' the girl snapped authoritatively.

'Now, Miz Maddy,' the one addressed answered easily. 'We ain't gonna hurt your l'il 'breed friend. We're just gonna learn him that he shouldn't go 'round talkin' to white gals.'

'Sure,' the one holding Bregan agreed. 'There's plenty o' Apache squaws he can bed down with. Ain't that right, redskin?' he asked of the boy, giving him a rough shake.

The shake nearly proved his undoing, because without replying Travis jerked his head back, unfortunately only catching his captor's cheek, rather than the man's nose which had been his intended target.

'Christ Almighty, you 'breed bastard,' Sol Barker snarled. 'You coulda broke my nose. Give him somethin' to think about, brother Breck.'

'My pleasure, brother Sol,' his companion replied, drawing back his fist to strike, despite Maddy Faulkener's insistent orders.

The blow never fell though, because before Barker could deliver it, something smashed into the area of his kidneys with sickening force, causing him to jerk his hands abruptly to the affected area and driving him to his knees.

Through the red mist of pain, Barker heard a sound and he listened unbelievingly.

Someone, somewhere, was whistling 'Shenandoah.'

4

Breck Barker staggered to his feet, pain slowly subsiding, as he turned to face this new threat.

Cord Wheeler was standing some three paces from the bigger man, leaning easily on his brass-knobbed cane.

'Three to one gives you a l'il mite the best of it, don't you think, suh?' Wheeler asked softly, his voice dropping into that easy New Orleans drawl. 'Why don't you try someone your own size, you stupid, ugly bastard?'

With a scream of incoherent rage, the big cowboy dropped his head and charged the man from El Paso. Wheeler waited until his attacker was almost touching him before slipping to one side and simultaneously slamming the heavy brass knob of his cane into Barker's solar plexus.

The big man's face turned red then grey as the pain knifed him. His suffering wasn't prolonged however, as in a smooth continuation of his first movement, Wheeler swept the cane upwards and, this time, slammed the knob into Barker's temple, dropping his victim like a stone.

Without apparently bothering to ascertain the effect of his blow, Wheeler pivoted easily, just in time to smash the cane's lead-weighted tip across the back of Sol Barker's neck as he blundered past.

The blow was clearly painful, but it failed to stop the enraged cowboy, who twisted clumsily and drove in at Wheeler again, hands reaching to grab.

Almost casually, Wheeler tossed his cane aside, stepped between Barker's reaching arms and hammered two swift punches into the cowboy's face. Barker rocked backwards then lunged in again, to meet Wheeler's knee driving upwards.

Almost vomiting in his agony, Barker jerked forwards grabbing desperately at the affected area, only to meet Wheeler's knee for a second time smashing into his nose and removing any interest he might have had in subsequent events.

Wheeler stepped back from his last victim, bending fluidly to lift his cane, as Maddy Faulkener screamed, 'Reese, NO!' her voice almost drowned by the crack of a pistol.

Wheeler's bend became a swift dive as, ignoring his cane, he rolled into the dirt palming the big Smith and Wesson and firing twice almost in a single movement.

Caught in the act of firing again, the two-gun man on the steps of the saloon seemed almost to throw his gun away as his body was driven backwards against the sundried boards by the impact of Wheeler's bullets.

Standing behind and to the side of Wheeler's opponent, a middle-sized cowboy, plainly his companion, was surreptitiously reaching for one of the silver-mounted Colts in his belt when a cold voice said, 'Leave it, Wade, or we'll be buryin' you along with Reese.'

★ ★ ★

'Hell Cord, you fight like an Apache,' Al Bregan growled, as Joe Ironhand unceremoniously pushed the last of the surviving Flying F cowhands on to his horse.

'I ain't forgettin' this, Bregan . . . ' Wade Dixon, the Flying F's *segundo*, began with a snarl.

'I ain't either,' the old peace officer interrupted coldly. 'Likewise, I ain't fergittin' I had to stop you shootin' Cord in the back.'

'You're scum, Wade, just plain scum,' Bregan went on dispassionately. 'You ain't fit to be mixed with the piss that run outta your mother's kennel. An' if you got any ideas about usin' that pistol, why fill your hand, you snake-eyed bastard.'

For a moment, it seemed that Dixon would comply, then the tension oozed out of him and he turned his pony with a savage jerk and led the way out of town.

Watching the four horsemen out of sight, the last leading the tarpaulin-wrapped body of Wheeler's victim, the man from El Paso turned to Bregan and said mildly, 'You'll understand, I don't make a habit of shootin' people I don't know, but I didn't get time for an introduction. Who was that feller?'

'Rides or rather rode for Dale Faulkener,' Ironhand grunted, 'and Al's wrong. You don't fight like an Apache. An Indian'd have left both them bastards dead.'

'Hell, say I saved the town the price o' two funerals,' Wheeler answered cynically. 'Judgin' from the men who ride for him,' he went on, 'I'd say this Faulkener ain't that choosy about the way he gets what he wants.'

'And you'd be about as wrong as you can be,' Bregan answered emphatically 'Dale Faulkener's a lot o' things but a back-shooter ain't one o' them. If he'd been here, Faulkener would ha' shot Reese hisself,' he finished grimly.

'It's true, Cord,' the old Apache averred. 'Drew Faulkener ain't got much time for Al an' me, but he's straight. Straight as a string.'

Wheeler confined himself to a disbelieving grunt.

*   *   *

Returning to the sheriff's house, Wheeler and his companions found Dallas bathing a long gash on her brother's head, while Maddy Faulkener held a bowl of hot water.

'What in hell happened to you, boy?' his uncle demanded.

'Sol Barker knocked him down before he tried to jump Cord,' Dallas Bregan explained absently, intent upon her brother's scalp.

'Looks clean at least,' Bregan offered, but Wheeler could see his hands tremble as he gently examined the boy's scalp.

'It is now, thanks to Dallas,' Maddy snapped, before demanding, 'Where are my father's riders, Sheriff?'

'They drifted on home,' Bregan responded easily. 'Travis, Miz Maddy, like you to meet a friend of mine, Cord Wheeler of El Paso.'

'I saw Mr Wheeler in action in the street,' the girl responded waspishly, 'and I must say, Mr Bregan, I find it hard to believe that you, of all people, would be in the company of gunmen.'

'I carry a gun, Miss Faulkener,' Wheeler responded mildly, ''cause in my line o' work I'd be long dead if'n I didn't. But I don't sell my gun,' he went on, voice taking on an edge. 'And you know very well that makes a difference.'

'I, for one,' Travis Bregan began, extending a slim hand, 'am sure glad Mr Wheeler happened along when he did. Them Barker boys have been known to play for keeps!'

'Glad I was around,' Wheeler assured the young man. 'And you better make that Cord.'

'Glad to,' Travis assured him heartily, before getting gingerly to his feet although not without a grimace.

'And now if you'll all excuse me,' the young man went on, 'me and Doc've got pressing business at the Hartmores.'

'Can't it wait, Travis?' Maddy Faulkener demanded, and her heart was in her eyes and voice. 'Surely the Hartmores will understand that you can't come with your head split open?'

'It's just a graze, Miz Madeline,' the boy responded, but his eyes were soft as he looked at the girl. 'And while I'm sure ol' Jesse Hartmore'd be glad to wait, what looks set to be their newest addition sure won't,' he finished with a grin, which widened considerably as Maddy Faulkener blushed the colour of a cactus rose.

* * *

The general store, and usually its owner, are often the best sources of information about a small town, unless you're looking for its bad characters, then the saloon is always the place to go.

Being well aware of both these facts, Wheeler limped awkwardly across the threshold of Cartuna's Mercantile Emporium later the same afternoon.

He paused at the wide counter, crowded with the oddments necessary even to frontier life and addressed the rotund, little man wearing a wide smile who stood behind the counter.

'I'm needin' a box o' Lucifers,' he began, returning the other's grin and settling himself on the lid of a convenient keg.

'That'll be one thin dime,' the other responded, sliding the box across the counter. 'Need anything to light with them matches? Got some real fine cigars,' the little man went on shrewdly. 'Better'n them horse droppin's you'll buy at the saloon.'

'Thank you, suh, I'm fixed for smokin',' Wheeler answered courteously. 'And Al Bregan told me to be careful, 'cause given the chance you'd sell me the whole store, buildin' an' all.'

'You a friend o' Al's?' the little man enquired, after his laughter at Bregan's apt description had subsided.

'Sure,' Wheeler responded, tendering his name and hand together. 'I'm guessin' you'll be Mr Olsen, the owner.'

'Given name Gus,' the little man responded smilingly, 'but everyone in town calls me 'Stretch'.'

'So what'd people around town think about these killin's?' Wheeler asked inconsequentially after a couple of minutes' desultory conversation.

'Well, the women are mostly real scared,' Olsen began judicially. 'So are most of the men, at least for their womenfolk. Ain't that right, Hamish?' Olsen demanded as a tall, broad-shouldered young man with red hair staggered through the rear doorway and dropped his burden with a relieved grunt.

'Aye, everyone's scared right enough,' the young man agreed readily, although Wheeler caught a flicker of something else behind the fierce blue eyes.

'Hard to see what Millie Graham and the Krantz girl mighta had in common . . . ' the detective began playing a hunch.

'They had nothing in common, ye damn fool!' the young Scotsman erupted. 'The first one was a bloody whore and Sarah was . . . Sarah was . . . ' he lapsed into incoherent muttering while Olsen said quickly, 'Finish with them air-tights Hamish! I want them on the shelves before dinner.'

The young man's only answer was a grunt but Wheeler caught the glare in his direction as the Scot turned away and the gold flash of the crucifix that the boy wore round his neck. Wheeler settled himself back comfortably on the nail keg, with a satisfied smile.

So. Now he knew who Sarah Krantz's secret admirer was and why she desperately needed to keep his identity a secret. But he was still no nearer to knowing or even guessing why these apparently completely unrelated women had all been murdered in the same way and left with that bizarre trademark. And as for Sarah Krantz's beau . . .

'No,' the man from El Paso assured himself, after the briefest moment of thought. 'Not in cold blood. And them murders was planned, for certain.'

Abruptly, Wheeler jerked himself out of his reverie and off the nail keg, before demanding of the surprised store keeper, 'Where'd I find Milt Gilmore's office, Stretch?'

Gilmore wasn't in his office, but the neatly lettered note, which was fastened to his door said, 'I'm round back,' and Wheeler simply followed his nose.

The office backed on to the main street of the little town and a short walk down the sundried flight of stairs fixed to the outside of the building led Wheeler into a small, dusty courtyard.

Glancing up and back, he noticed that the back window of the office overlooked the street and the front door of the jail, while facing him was a neat wooden shed, recently erected and on the door of which was pinned a notice which said simply: 'Keep out'.

Carefully, Wheeler tried the handle only to leap back as a voice screamed pettishly, 'Get the hell away from there!'

Wheeler was kept waiting only a moment, when the door was wrenched open and an irate young man stuck his face out.

'What in hell d'you want, cowboy?' the owner of the face snarled menacingly.

5

'I'm bettin' you're Mr Milt Gilmore ain't you?' Wheeler drawled mildly, slipping easily into his role of a Southern gentleman, afflicted with a terminal case of mild stupidity.

'And if I am?' Gilmore snapped.

'Well,' Wheeler began easily, 'your daddy, Mr Hank Gilmore, advised me to look you up, on account of he said you might be able to help me with somethin', suh.'

'Well . . . oh Goddammit, you better come in, I suppose!' Gilmore snapped ungraciously.

'Sure obliged,' Wheeler responded, clumsily dropping his hat as he crossed the threshold. Reaching down, Wheeler retrieved his headgear, while, at the same time, bringing his face close to the jamb of the door.

For a moment he scrutinized the

woodwork, before straightening to find Milt Gilmore regarding him suspiciously.

'So what was it you wanted, Mr . . . ?' the lawyer began warily.

'I'm helpin' Sheriff Bregan with this here murder that happened a few days ago,' Wheeler began, after supplying his name and occupation. 'And your daddy seemed to think you might be able to help me, seein' as how you do so much law business around town.'

'My father,' Gilmore began sneeringly, 'should know better!

'He is well aware that I have no interest in criminal law,' the lawyer went on pompously. 'And, further-more, I don't have very much at all to do with the riff-raff that live in this Godforsaken hole!'

'Well, I guess that's pretty definite,' Wheeler responded mildly. 'Say,' he went on, looking around, 'why ain't this place got no windows?'

'Because I use it as a darkroom,'

Gilmore snapped impatiently, his chiselled lips working petulantly. 'Didn't my esteemed father tell you that my hobby is photography?'

'Nope,' Wheeler admitted, truthfully for once, 'he sure never mentioned it. Is that your camera?' he went on innocently, stepping neatly past the lawyer and approaching the object he'd spotted standing resplendent on a brass-mounted tripod.

'For Christ's sake, don't touch,' Gilmore snapped nervously, as Wheeler stretched out a hand. 'It's very delicate.'

'Oh sure,' Wheeler grinned vacantly, although his quick eyes had already detected one or two non-standard features of what was plainly Gilmore's prize possession.

'Why ain't there no cap on the front, Mr Gilmore?' Wheeler asked innocently, as the lawyer came to stand next to his camera.

'Special design of my own,' Gilmore explained, pride working its way past suspicion. 'I got tired of standing in front so I had this device fitted,' he went on, indicating a lever mechanism which extended along the body of the camera. 'Just pull this lever and the plate starts exposing. It means I can stay behind the camera and watch what I'm photographing while the picture's being taken.'

'Sure sounds like a bang-up idea,' Wheeler admitted, although his agile mind was already considering the numerous advantages a camera of that type might have for the owner of a high-class brothel.

After a few more desultory questions, Wheeler took his courteous leave and, with his visitor gone, Gilmore sat down and waited for a full ten minutes by the ornate gold watch he wore on a chain across his narrow vest.

At the end of that time he rose silently and twitched back the curtain which separated the tiny storage area from the rest of the room.

'You can come out now, Dixon,' he snapped, as a man stumbled out of his makeshift hiding place, almost gagging from the smell of the chemicals stored there.

'What in hell did that son of a bitch want?' the *segundo* of the Flying F grated, when he finally found himself capable of speech once again.

'Surprisingly enough, he didn't tell me,' came the waspish response, muffled slightly, since Gilmore had eased open the door and was minutely examining the area of the frame which had caught Wheeler's interest.

'Dammit,' the lawyer snarled, jerking upright, before demanding, 'What colour was that Sadler woman's dress?'

'I . . . I . . . ' Dixon spluttered.

'Never mind,' Gilmore sneered, cutting his companion off abruptly. 'I've got a feeling Mr Clever Wheeler is a little too smart for our good,' he went on, after a moment's thought. 'See Castro before you leave tonight and arrange a little . . . accident.'

'Sure,' Dixon responded fulsomely. 'Leave it to me, Milt, there won't be no..'

'No slip ups were you about to say, Mr . . . Hardin?' Gilmore snapped, sneering as the other flinched as if at a blow.

'It's too late, there already has been,' the lawyer went on, thin, handsome face contracting into a devilish smile. 'And another failure might prove . . . unfortunate . . . for you! I'm not sure I can pull you clear of another mess, Mr . . . Dixon,' the lawyer finished, with a spiteful laugh, clearly revelling in his power to hurt.

'Now get out,' Gilmore snapped. 'And don't forget about Castro!'

Without another word and nursing a hatred in his heart almost too big to bear, Dixon slouched through the door and, with a swift look right and left, darted down an adjacent alley leading away from Cartuna's main street.

And moments later, although now there was no one to hear, a thin melody came drifting around the corner of the building which housed Gilmore's office. Someone, somewhere, was whistling 'Shenandoah'.

★　★　★

'Sure a nice night for a walk,' Wheeler assured himself, before adding, 'Wonder why them two *hombres* are trying to spoil it?'

Wheeler was making his way back to the better of Cartuna's two hotels where he had rented a room, after a late visit to the saloon, by taking a short-cut through what passed for the town's Mexican quarter.

Within minutes of entering the moon-shadowed streets, the hairs on the back of his neck had begun to prickle and, obedient to the signal, Wheeler had abruptly paused to light a cigar he didn't want.

Caught unexpectedly in the flare of the match, two shadows had hurriedly ducked into a convenient alley, leaving Wheeler to continue his walk in a far more pensive frame of mind.

★   ★   ★

'I don' like this, Julio,' Jaco whined nervously. 'He don' act like no gringo I ever kill before.'

'Idiot!' his more courageous friend snarled. 'Gringos are all the same; easy meat for the picking! This one is goin' home the long way, that is all.'

'Now, you go there,' he ordered, imperiously indicating the space between the town's only livery stable and its ramshackle corral which Cord Wheeler had limped slowly into just moments before. 'While I get in front of him. This is gonna be ver' easy, Jaco, *mi compadre*. After all, what can one cripple do against two of us?'

Leaving his companion to follow the man from El Paso down the maze of side streets which would lead them both eventually back to Wheeler's hotel, Julio sprinted silently past the corral and down a couple of convenient alleys before hiding himself behind the corner of the general store, near where his victim would have to emerge in order to re-enter Main Street and thus make his way to his hotel.

Seconds dragged into minutes and

Julio had just begun to wonder if perhaps cowardly little Jaco had raised enough guts to do the killing himself, when a dark figure moved hesitantly out of the shadows and began to approach the lighter area of Main Street.

Silhouetted against the moonlight Julio could clearly make out the gringo's flat crowned hat and neat broadcloth coat. Despite the garments there was something different about the figure and as Julio lifted his pistol and fired, he suddenly realized what it was. The man he had shot and who was lying dead or badly wounded just inside the entrance to the alley had no limp!

He had barely risen to his feet, realization of his mistake dawning, when a razor-sharp blade pricked him in the throat, just over the big, throbbing artery and a cold voice said softly, in fluent Border Spanish, 'Just ease that pistol back here, *mi amigo*, then we'll go see how your li'l friend's doin'.'

Al Bregan had just risen from the battered old flat-topped desk in the far corner of his combined jail and office, prior to his nightly rounds, when the street door was pushed open and a greasy, evil-visaged Mexican erupted into the room, to land sprawling on the dusty boards. Moments later, a grim-faced Cord Wheeler followed him more sedately, only to find himself looking into the bore of a Colt .45, held in Bregan's rock-steady fist.

'Jesus, Cord, you sure know how to make an entrance!' the old peace officer rasped, as he fluidly holstered the pistol and Joe Ironhand rose from his crouch by the door of the cells, easing the hammer of his Winchester carbine as he did so.

'Sure hope I didn't wake you, Al,' Wheeler began, a trifle more tightly than usual, and with a barely discernible wink at the Apache. 'This *hombre* and his *amigo* just tried to kill me and I thought mebbe we should ask them a few questions.'

'Sure,' Ironhand grunted, before Bregan could speak. 'I'll light the stove and sharpen up a coupla mesquite sticks. You figger we'll need this *hombre* alive after we get through askin'?'

'Can't see why,' Wheeler assured him. 'Only cost the county money to feed him. You might look at his friend while you're gettin' your stuff, Joe,' he went on. 'He's in the alley across the street and he may not bleed to death if you're real quick.'

'Now listen, *amigo*,' Wheeler began softly, after Ironhand had left and he'd propped the uninjured Mexican against the front of Bregan's desk. 'I ain't keen on lettin' that damn Apache loose on you, especially since I ain't had supper yet, but unless you tell me what I want to know, you ain't leavin' me much choice.'

'The sheriff,' Julio snapped, speaking good but accented English. 'Even this gringo sheriff will not allow this. Is against the law! Gringo law!'

'Now, Julio,' Bregan assured him, having quickly caught on to Wheeler's plan, 'you an' me've known each other a long time. Who d'you think's gonna worry what happens to a sorry son of a bitch like you? Fella whose payin' you?'

'Believe me,' the old man went on with relish, 'there ain't no amount of money gonna make up for what Joe'll do to you.'

For a moment, stark fear flamed in the Mexican's eyes, then, incredibly, he shook his head.

'I cannot,' he muttered. 'The man he is very powerful, very strong. If I tell and you let me live,' he went on with a sneer of disbelief, 'I won't live to get out of town.'

'Hell,' Wheeler said mildly 'if that's all your worried about, why, I figger the sheriff and me between us can figger out some way o' keepin' you safe. I got friends,' the detective went on, 'good friends, down below the Border; people who'd watch out for you, keep you safe, mebbe even give you a job.'

'Who, gringo?' Julio sneered. 'Who would a gringo know below the Border who has such power. Who of the great ones there?'

Without preamble, Wheeler leant forward and whispered briefly in the other's ear.

For a long moment, Julio stared aghast at the other.

'Him?' the Mexican finally managed to croak. 'But he hates gringos, all gringos like poison. No,' he went on, 'I don' believe you!'

'You're right about him hatin' gringos,' Wheeler agreed. 'But I done him a favour once long time ago, and he ain't the forgettin' sort. Take it or leave it, but it's about the only chance you got unless . . . ' the detective finished, jerking his head meaningly towards the door through which Joe Ironhand had departed.

So intent were Wheeler and Bregan on their prisoner, that neither saw the door, which Ironhand had left ajar, begin to slide open.

'OK,' Julio admitted grudgingly after a moment's rapid thought. 'I tell you who hire us, but you gotta keep that gringo bastard from . . .' The rest of his sentence was lost in the crack of a shot as, caught in the chest, the Mexican slumped lifeless to the floor.

6

There was a single moment of stunned silence, then Wheeler had catapulted himself across the room, to drop prone by the door, as Bregan slowed by age and bulk, blew out the lamp before lumbering back to crouch behind the desk.

'Stay where you are, Al,' Wheeler ordered softly as he began to ease back the door. 'He may not be finished yet.'

His words proved prophetic as, with the door barely halfway open, a bullet tore into the flimsy wooden frame at waist height.

'Bastard ain't foolin',' Wheeler told himself grimly, drawing his legs underneath him. 'Took time to aim for a gut shot too.'

Without warning Wheeler suddenly slammed the door back on its hinges, launching himself through the opening in almost the same movement and colliding with a dark figure making its hurried way towards the door of the jail.

Driven to fighting madness, Wheeler's iron grip was biting into his victim's throat when he felt his arms grabbed and Bregan's voice was saying, 'Cord, Cord! For Christ's sake, loosen up! It's Travis! You hear me! You're killin' Travis.'

★ ★ ★

'Sure hope you ain't hurt too much, son,' Wheeler offered diffidently, as he watched Travis Bregan trying to knead some feeling back into his talking apparatus.

'Not so you'd notice,' the youngster croaked with a desperate attempt at a grin. 'Jesus, Cord,' he went one 'you got a fair grip.'

'Comes from cowboying too long, I guess, when I was your age,' Wheeler admitted, helping the boy up from his father's battered office chair.

'What in hell was you doin' out there, boy?' Bregan demanded, irritable and suspicious. 'Ain't you got no more sense than to come runnin' when you hear shootin'?'

'I was headed this way, anyhow, Pa,' the boy bridled instantly. 'Figgered mebbe you or Joe mighta been hurt. Guess I shouldn't have bothered!'

'Can't blame the boy, Al,' Wheeler interposed quickly. 'He's just thinking like a doctor.'

For a long moment, Bregan glared back at the detective and past him to where Joe Ironhand was conspicuously examining the ceiling.

Then, the old peace officer sighed and ran a trembling hand through thinning iron-grey hair.

'Guess I must be losin' my wool at that, Cord. I'm sorry, boy,' he went on, this time addressing his son. 'These murders got me so jumpy ain't even sure which way is up anymore.'

'Sure, Pa,' Travis responded, instantly

contrite. 'Guess we're all a little that way. Cord,' he continued throatily, 'I was comin' this way to find you.'

Wheeler looked his surprise as the boy went on.

'Wade Dixon rode in just before dark with a message. From Dale Faulkener. He says he wants to see you. Tomorrow. Somethin' about it being to your advantage.'

★   ★   ★

Dawn found Wheeler astride a borrowed pony, pushing easily along the plain trail that led eventually to the Flying F.

'Take you good part of the day,' Joe Ironhand had assured him, after supplying the necessary directions and the tough little pony. ''Less you feel like pushin' that pony and, was I you, I wouldn't. Time to push a horse is when you're runnin' away,' he finished unnecessarily.

'Well, I'll try and remember that,

Granpa,' Wheeler responded with a grin. 'Anymore good advice?'

'Yeah,' Ironhand snapped. 'Don't forget Wade Dixon sure is fond of a back shot.'

Wheeler was pondering this last piece of good but superfluous advice when he had one of those pieces of good fortune which often marks the difference between a good detective and a great one.

Off the trail, under one of the interminable mesquites which dotted the slope past which he was riding, he caught a glint of something metallic where no such thing should have been.

Without slackening his pace, Wheeler allowed the little pony to move on for about 200 yards, before signalling a halt through the reins.

Having secured his mount to a convenient branch, Wheeler moved up the slope and skirted the area where the flash of light had caught his attention, his boots leaving no discernible marks on the loose shale of the slope.

The bush he was searching for was in a small cluster of three and having assured himself that none of them were being used by a snake for its afternoon siesta, Wheeler delved carefully in the soil where he estimated the flash of light to have originated. What he found came as something of a shock.

* * *

'And just what in hell are you doin' here?' Wheeler demanded of his find, which turned out to be a handsome, although much worn, Ingersoll pocketwatch. Carefully, the man from El Paso turned the silver case over and used a fingernail to pry open the case.

Inside, neatly engraved on the rear cover, were the words: 'To my dear son, John, on the occasion of his twenty-first birthday. All my love, Mother.'

Which left Wheeler with much food for thought as he went back up the trail to regain his patiently waiting mount.

Although, as it happened, this wasn't the biggest surprise of the day.

⋆ ⋆ ⋆

The Flying F turned out to be a largish cattle spread for that part of the country and the spacious dining-room of the big main house, into which Wheeler was shown upon his arrival, showed a woman's influence in its tasteful, though inexpensive decor.

Dale Faulkener was waiting for Wheeler in a big chair by the fireplace and he rose to greet his guest with a touch of old world courtesy.

'Mr Wheeler,' Faulkener began, extending a hand, his clipped tones at odds with the untidy work clothes he wore. 'Thank you for taking the trouble to come.'

'My pleasure, suh,' Wheeler assured him, before saying, 'I wasn't aware that you were an Englishman.'

'No reason why you should be, I suppose,' Faulkener began abruptly, although his mouth quickly softened into a smile. 'You'll excuse me, Mr Wheeler, I'm a little touchy on the subject. May I offer you a cigar?'

With a good smoke going to his satisfaction Wheeler found himself politely ushered into a seat across from the owner of the Flying F.

'I'm not one to beat about the bush, Mr Wheeler,' the latter began, 'I have something of a problem and I'm hoping you're the man to solve it for me.'

'It depends on the problem,' Wheeler responded mildly. 'But before you go any further, I told your daughter and now I'm tellin' you: my gun ain't for sale.'

'I'm pleased to hear it,' Faulkener assured him. 'I don't want your gun, but I was thinking about hiring you!'

'As you probably know,' Faulkener went on before a very startled Cord Wheeler had had time to collect his thoughts, 'the cattle business hasn't been so good for a number of years. It's got so bad that me and the little ranches around here can't even raise expense money from the bank. So . . . '

'You've gotta sell cows,' Wheeler interrupted. 'It's the same all over,' he went on. 'But it can't last. Leastwise, that's what I been hearin'.'

'Damn right, it can't last,' Faulkener assured him 'Next spring prices look set to sky rocket. If me and the rest can just last 'til then, why, we're home clear.'

'Sounds like it might be a good time for a big operation like this to pick up a coupla them little spreads dirt cheap,' Wheeler offered slyly.

'Those men are my neighbours,' Faulkener began hotly. 'Their blood's in this land, just like mine and. .' he paused, confused by Wheeler's grin, then he relaxed. 'All right, you found out what you wanted to know?' Faulkener demanded softly.

'Al Bregan an' his deppity said you was straight, suh,' Wheeler began with a shrug. 'But I don't let nobody make up my mind about anyone for me.'

'And what have you decided?' Faulkener snapped.

'Well . . . I'm still listening,' came the mild reply.

'Like I was saying,' Faulkener resumed, after a moment's thought. 'Cattle business is sure to boom again soon and we just got to get through 'til then. I'm puttin' together a trail herd, the best stock me and Jenkins o' the Circle Q and a few others can get together and we're planning to drive to the railhead at Videlio. If we can make it, there's a buyer there who'll take the steers at a fair price and we'll all have a good chance to come through.'

'Seems like a good proposition to me,' Wheeler said. 'Where do I come in?'

'Between here and the railhead is 500 miles of the worst country in the West. It's infested with bandits and Border scum of all sorts. We can't go round it and the drive's got to get through or none of us'll last six months. I've got another reason, too,' Faulkener added quietly. 'The Flying F's mortgaged to the hilt. I've got to pay off and this drive is my only chance.'

'Sounds like you need a railroad spur, more than a drive trail,' Wheeler offered.

'Sure,' Faulkener agreed. 'It'd make sense, for us and for the ranches further south. There was some talk about it,' the old man finished, 'but it never came to anything that I heard of.'

'Anyhow,' the old cow man went on, 'that aside, for now, I need a good man, a man who don't scare,' Faulkener finished bluntly. 'And after that little show in town the other day, I'm sayin' you're him.'

'I'll go with you, suh,' Wheeler said slowly, after a long pause during which he had been thinking furiously. 'But I figger I'm gonna need a little help.'

★ ★ ★

'Cord, I wouldn't be no use to you,' Joe Ironhand said bluntly, having heard

Wheeler's proposition.

'Why in hell not?' the man from El Paso demanded. 'I know you ain't scared.'

Wheeler had returned to Cartuna after a night spent at the Faulkener ranch, and immediately found the old Apache and explained the problem.

Shaken out of his customary equanimity, Wheeler went on.

'I figger, like you, that Faulkener's straight, but there's something back o' this whole business that I can't figger.

'Dixon and that smooth-talking bastard Gilmore are in it up to their necks,' Wheeler went on. 'And that means it ain't just some evil son of a bitch who gets his kicks from killin' women who can't fight back.

'I need a good man to back me up and . . . '

'Look up the saloon there,' Ironhand interrupted. 'What do you see?'

Without comprehending, Wheeler flicked his gaze up the dusty street and said simply, 'Two horses on the rail outside, coupla cowboys in chairs and not much else. What's your point?'

'D'you know what I can see?' Iron-hand asked softly and when Wheeler didn't answer, he went on, 'Just a big blur. Up to about six feet away, I'm OK. Past that, I can't see nothin'.'

'I'm guessin' you don't want that generally known,' Wheeler suggested, after a long pause.

'Damn right,' the old Indian assured him with some asperity. 'And you can see why I ain't gonna be no use to you.'

'Guess I'll just have to chance it by myself,' Wheeler responded, although with little enthusiasm. 'Sure don't like my chances, though.'

'Why not take Travis?' Ironhand suggested. 'Taught him myself, he's a good man. And it wouldn't hurt for him and Maddy Faulkener to spend a little time around each other,' the old man finished slyly.

'Mebbe,' Wheeler agreed reluctantly. 'Afore I forget, do something else for me, will you?'

'Sure,' the other agreed instantly. 'What is it?'

'Ask Hank Gilmore to dig the bullet outta that Greaser and see if you can match it to a pistol,' came the surprising answer.

7

Dawn found Wheeler and Travis Bregan jogging easily along the plain trail from Cartuna to the Flying F.

Travis had agreed readily enough to his uncle's suggestion, although there seemed a studied reluctance in his demeanour which Wheeler noted with some concern.

'How'd you come to get interested in doctoring?' Wheeler asked cautiously, after they had been riding for some hours.

'Oh,' Travis began, clearly jerked back to reality by Wheeler's question. 'Guess I've just always wanted to help people. Seen a lot o' folk pass on when just a simple thing would've saved them. Didn't want to see that happen no more.'

'Sounds like a good way to spend your life,' Wheeler offered lamely and when the boy didn't respond, the detective said bluntly, 'Travis, son, have you got somethin' against makin' this trip with me?

''Cause if you have, boy,' he went on, 'I'd sooner you'd spit it out, rather than sit there like some sick dogie!'

'It ain't you, or the trip that bothers me,' Bregan blurted out. 'It's . . . it's . . . it's . . . Maddy Faulkener,' he managed, before lapsing into a resentful silence.

'You mebbe don't like her?' Wheeler suggested artlessly.

'Don't like her!' Travis bridled instantly. 'Why, I'd . . . '

He stopped in a welter of confusion and Wheeler said gently, 'Guess mebbe you'd better tell me about it.'

' . . . and that's about it, Cord,' Bregan finished hesitantly. 'I've loved her since we were in school, but every time I tried to talk to her or even get near her, Charlie, that damn brother of hers, got in the way. So I quit tryin'.'

'What about her? How does she feel about you?' Wheeler asked gently.

'I don't know,' the boy admitted with a miserable shrug. 'I thought once ... mebbe ... but now she's engaged to Milt Gilmore, least that's the talk, and I guess I ain't got a chance.'

'Don't bet too high on that,' Wheeler assured him, having seen the look in Madelaine Faulkener's eyes while Dallas had been cleaning her brother's cut head. 'And don't you be too quick making her mind up for her,' he finished decisively, seeing the beginnings of argument on the other's face.

* * *

The rest of the trip to the Faulkener ranch passed without incident and as Wheeler and his companion swung down in front of the big horse corral, Wheeler motioned the boy towards him, before saying in a normal tone of voice, 'Best if you and me mebbe ain't too friendly on this here trip,' Wheeler cautioned. 'I'm gonna need you watchin' my back and if people think we ain't that keen on each other, well they just may let somethin' slip. So don't go takin' offence at anything I say, *sabe*?'

'Sure, Cord,' the young man murmured instantly replacing his grin with a look of sullen indifference as he turned back to his mount.

'Afore we go,' Wheeler went on easily, falling in beside Travis as they made their way to the main house, and drawing the watch he had found the previous day from a pocket of his greasy buckskin jacket. 'You ever see this before?'

'Perhaps,' Bregan admitted slowly after a careful examination of the battered Ingersoll. 'There was a friend of Milt Gilmore's, came from back East, name of Joe . . . no John something . . . can't remember his last name. He sure had a watch like that.'

'Ever hear anything else about him?' Wheeler asked.

'No.' Bregan began, before memory stirred and he said, 'Wait up. Yeah, I remember now. He said he worked for the railroad.'

'What happened to him?' Wheeler asked softly.

'Don't rightly know,' Travis admitted, puzzlement creasing his brow. 'One day he just weren't around no more. Musta gone back East.'

* * *

Faulkener wasn't in the house and it was a dishevelled Madison Faulkener who answered the door.

'Oh, Mr Wheeler' she began, tone distinctly uncordial, until she spotted Travis, at which point woman-like, her hands flew to her hair.

'Come in, won't you,' she fluttered, swiftly removing her apron and smoothing her dress, although her eyes barely left the unsmiling face of the youth at Wheeler's side.

'Pa's with the herd,' she began with a rush. 'Said he'd be there for the rest of the day. Why don't you wait here for him?'

'Well, that's right nice of you, Miz Faulkener,' Wheeler began, knowing the invitation wasn't for his benefit. 'But I figger I just better get straight to work. No call for him to come though,' he added, jerking a contemptuous thumb in Bregan's direction.

'You better stay here with Miz Faulkener,' Wheeler snapped abruptly. 'Mebbe she can find a use for you, dustin' and such,' he added with a sneer and a surreptitious wink. ''Cause I sure as hell don't see how I'm gonna be able to.'

*　*　*

Wheeler found the drive herd under a billowing cloud of dust, a bare mile from the ranch buildings.

'Is this all we're taking?' he asked, having located Faulkener astride a big raw-boned cowhorse, near where a couple of hard-working cowhands were operating the eight cow branding chute.

'This is about half our cut,' Faulkener explained. 'Wade and the boys have been making another gather on the west range;

should have 'em here by nightfall.'

'How long before you're ready to drive?' Wheeler bellowed, almost choking in the dust and the smoke thrown up by the rapidly applied branding irons.

'With the chutes, we'll have finished with our bunch by the afternoon. Circle Q and the rest of the boys'll be drivin' in the next day or day after that, dependin' how their roundups've gone,' Faulkener offered.

'Chutes sure make life easy,' Wheeler admitted. 'So, say a day after that for the boys to pick their strings and fix up the chuck wagon. We can start in about three days?'

'Sure,' Faulkener agreed. 'You got some reason to be anxious to go, Cord?'

'Nope,' Wheeler admitted, 'but I want a coupla days to look over the country we'll be drivin' through. Best if'n you lay out the trail for me now, I guess.'

'Pleased too,' Faulkener agreed.

★ ★ ★

Squatting on the ground, cowboy style, Faulkener picked up a discarded twig and began to make a rapid sketch.

'First coupla days we'll be trailing across Flying F land,' he began, 'until we reach the mountains.'

'We mebbe carrying the cows across, suh?' Wheeler asked interestedly.

'Oh they ain't really mountains,' Faulkener went on. 'Just a low range of hills the local Mexicans call 'little Mesa'. And there's a good pass, Snake Pass, that runs through them. Flat wide, real easy drivin'.'

'This the only way through them hills?' Wheeler asked thoughtfully.

'Sure is,' he was informed. 'They ain't big but they're certainly mean.'

'And this pass, it's on your land?' Wheeler went on.

'Certainly. I filed on part of the range which had the pass because the source of the Blanco is there, that's the river that waters the eastern range,' Faulkener explained. 'Glad I did too,' he went on, 'when I found that there was no other way over the little Mesa within a hundred miles.'

'A hundred miles?' Wheeler echoed.

'Sure,' Faulkener assured him. 'If you don't use Snake Pass, you got to drive a hundred miles north and then south again to go round them and get back on the only trail to Videlio. And it's real bad country, no water and sand desert where it isn't salt pan.'

Wheeler nodded absently, adding another little piece to the picture of the case which was forming in his mind.

* * *

'So how'd you make out with Miz Maddy yesterday?' Wheeler asked whimsically, as he and Travis negotiated the trail away from the Flying F ranch house in the chill pre-dawn light.

'I'd as soon have to do with a Gila monster!' came the snapped reply. 'Though I gotta say,' Bregan added, with a grin, 'I can't remember when I've enjoyed arguing quite so much with anyone!'

'What was you arguing about?' Wheeler asked absently, eyes intent upon the ground before him and to the left.

'Her choice of fiancé!' the youngster snapped. 'I told her Uncle Joe figgers Gilmore's a bad one and since he can smell a rattler at about 100 feet, I said I thought his opinion was good.' Bregan paused, before saying disconsolately, 'And we just kinda took it from there. I'm guessin' she'll probably never speak to me again.'

'I doubt if you'll be that lucky,' Wheeler told him cynically.

The trail the two men were following soon began to climb gently and after a couple of hour's steady riding, Wheeler turned in his saddle and said, 'How far you figger we are from the main house, Travis?'

'Twelve, mebbe fifteen miles,' the other grunted, without hesitation.

'So call it a day's drive,' Wheeler responded thoughtfully.

'I wouldn't know, Cord,' the boy

admitted frankly. 'Never had much to do with ranch work.'

Wheeler nodded absently as the boy edged up next to him and asked simply, indicating the ground in front of his pony's hoofs, 'Cord, you got some reason to be trailin' these four *hombres*?'

'You noticed,' Wheeler said simply. 'What do you make of it?' he went on, indicating the faint hoofmarks that he had been following, with difficulty, for the last hour.

'They're pretty old,' Travis began, having slid from his pony and squatted by the trail. 'Two, mebbe three months. Four men, shod ponies. They're white men and one of them ain't used to riding. No,' he went on, walking back along the faint line of prints, 'that ain't all of it. He ain't used to horses but the one he's riding is being led.'

'Mount up,' Wheeler ordered. 'Which way they headed?'

'Straight north,' Travis grunted. 'Looks like they was headin' for Snake Pass.'

For most of that long dusty day, Wheeler and his companion followed the faint trail, heading north and following the gently rising ground that led to the uplands and the pass through the hills.

Less than an hour of daylight remained when Wheeler pulled his mount abruptly to a halt and pointed to a little flat clearing some hundred yards ahead, saying softly, 'Looks like they camped. Let's take a look.'

'Like I said,' Travis began, 'four men. One wearin' town boots, one with cowboy boots, and the other two with Mex boots and them big rowelled spurs. All pretty young by their walks, no old men but the fella with the town boots is awful tired. Oh and he had his hands tied behind his back.'

'All four ride away in the morning?' Wheeler asked, although he'd made his own assessment of the tracks.

'Sure,' Travis assured him. 'And they was all ridin',' the boy went on seeing what was behind Wheeler's question.

'None o' them ponies was carrying dead weight.'

'Recognize any of the tracks?' Wheeler asked, rising to scan the low slope which extended away from the camp ground, illuminated now by the rays of the setting sun.

'No, but . . . ' Travis began, only to find himself suddenly grabbed and flung off his feet as the report of a shot rang out and a bullet snapped viciously from a rock six feet behind them.

8

Without speaking, Wheeler wriggled quickly back across the clearing, followed closely by Bregan, to where they had concealed their mounts in a fold of rock which hid them from the marksman on the higher ground.

Bregan swiftly pulled his battered Winchester from its saddle boot and having assured himself that there was a round in the chamber, began to move back towards the clearing.

'Where you goin'?' Wheeler demanded.

'I don't like bein' shot at,' came the waspish reply. 'I figger the *hombre* up in them rocks wants discouragin' some.'

'Just wait up, Travis,' Wheeler suggested. 'Try usin' your head. Listen.'

In the pre-dusk stillness of the desert, faint but unmistakable, came the sound of hoofbeats fading, even as the two men listened, into nothingness and distance.

'Long gone,' Wheeler stated bluntly. 'We'll find a place to camp for tonight and look for tracks in the morning.'

'We better get movin', Cord,' Bregan offered. 'If we want to find a place before nightfall.'

'No need,' Wheeler assured his companions 'I figger yonder is as good a place as any.'

'But . . . but, hell, Cord, supposin' that *hombre* comes back! We wouldn't . . . ' the youngster began.

'You wasn't listenin' good,' Wheeler interrupted mildly. 'There was two o' them and they won't be back. Cowardly skunks are probably halfway to Mexico by now. Get your bedroll and break out that fry pan. I'm hungry.'

Darkness had fallen with characteristic desert swiftness and the moon was barely rising over the camp, with its two peacefully sleeping occupants, when the night was shattered by the roar of gunfire and the two blanket-wrapped bundles by the fire jerked as bullets slammed into them.

Seconds passed with no movement from the bodies by the fire and then two dark forms slipped, swift and silent, across the clearing.

The first killer halted by the blanket-shrouded body of his victim, disdainfully pushing a boot under the corpse to enable him to turn it over for a closer inspection.

The body shifted easily, too easily, and a look of vacant surprise replaced the bearded Mexican's vicious grin as he found himself looking down at a neatly tied bundle of mesquite branches.

His surprise was not allowed to last long.

'*Saludos, amigos*,' a soft voice said close behind him.

'Get rid of the guns, *amigos*,' the voice went on in easy accentless Border Spanish. 'Very slowly. And stand very still while you're doing it.'

'I don' think we gonna do that,' the bearded one sneered, turning carefully and keeping his hands at waist height as his scarfaced friend followed his example, at the same time moving slowly away, out of the firelight.

The two Mexicans found themselves confronted by the lone figure of Cord Wheeler, his pistol holstered and right hand thumb-hooked into his worn gunbelt.

'Where is your friend, *amigo*?' the scarfaced one asked, almost sympathetically, as he continued his slow sideways move taking him out of Wheeler's immediate arch of vision.

'You'll do just about there, pigface!' Wheeler snapped, turning slightly to bring himself equidistant between the two men, his words freezing the scarfaced bandit into immediate immobility.

'An if it's any of your business,' Wheeler went on, 'I'm guessin' one of you bastards killed him this afternoon.'

'That is ver' sad, *amigo*,' the bearded Mexican said softly. 'Mebbe you better go see him,' and level with his last word the *bandido* sent a hand driving for his holstered Colt.

Cord Wheeler's first shot smashed into the bearded one's chest before the Mexican's pistol had even cleared leather and his second took the man between the eyes as Wheeler snapped into a desperate roll away from the firelight, triggering his third shot in the direction of the second bandit.

Caught in the head and chest, the scarfaced one jerked backwards, trying desperately to raise his pistol, before flopping into the sand stone dead.

For a long moment the clearing was still, then Wheeler wriggled round behind the body of his first victim. When nothing happened, he moved carefully backwards to where Travis was patiently waiting, a fresh round jacked into the breech of his Winchester.

'Wait here, I'm gonna check around,' the man from El Paso grated.

Minutes later, a whippoorwill called from the edge of the clearing and Wheeler walked into the firelight as Travis moved forward to join him.

'Jesus, Cord,' the boy began lost in

admiration. 'That was the best shootin'
I've ever seen in my life.'

'The worst,' Wheeler corrected sourly.
'I was tryin to get one of them alive!'

★ ★ ★

Morning showed the tracks left by the
two Mexicans leading to their patiently
waiting ponies.

'Either of these two belong to the
ones we was trackin' before?' Wheeler
asked, as he swung aboard his mount
and headed the tough little mustang
towards Snake Pass,

'Don't think so,' Travis offered
uncertainly. 'These two are sure both
wearing the right sorta spurs,' he went
on, pointing to where Wheeler had left
the bodies, his only response to
Bregan's request for burial having been.
'Why? Do you think they'd have
planted us? 'Sides, buzzards has to eat.'

'But them tracks was awful faint,' the
youngster finished, white-faced and
steadfastly keeping his gaze from the

ominous black shapes which were beginning to circle in the clear blue sky.

It wasn't until later that day, after Wheeler had satisfied himself about the first few days' trail conditions and they had left Snake Pass a couple of miles behind them, that Travis Bregan got around to asking about something that Maddy Faulkener had pushed far to the back of his mind.

'Cord, I can't figger why you're makin' this trip,' the boy stated bluntly.

'I'm still workin' on your dad's murder case,' Wheeler returned mildly. 'I'm playin' a hunch,' the man from El Paso went on carefully. 'I know Dixon and Gilmore are mixed up together somehow, and I'm pretty sure they murdered Miz Sadler. There's somethin' else back of it too, that I ain't quite figgered out yet, but there's one thing that connects it all.'

'What's that?' the boy demanded.

'Maddy Faulkener's got blonde hair and so did all the victims,' Wheeler offered softly.

'What!' Bregan snapped. 'You don't figger they might . . . '

'I'm here, ain't I?' came the cold retort.

★ ★ ★

Earlier that day, someone else had been developing his interest in the daughter of the owner of the Flying F.

Milt Gilmore had arrived at the door of the ranch house dressed for riding, and before she had quite decided what to do, Madelaine Faulkener had found herself on a horse jogging easily along beside the lawyer.

Gilmore rode badly and it wasn't long before he suggested a halt in the shade of some cottonwoods bordering a tiny stream.

'I've come out today for a particular reason, Madelaine, my dear,' he began fulsomely.

'We've been engaged for some months now,' Gilmore went on, 'and I think its about time we named the day.

People are starting to talk, you know.'

'Are they?' Maddy stammered, jerked out of a reverie that involved black hair and grey eyes, both of which belonged to Travis Bregan.

'Why yes,' Gilmore responded with a patronizing smile. 'Won't you at least think about it, dear?'

'Right now isn't the best time,' Maddy prevaricated. 'With the drive an' all . . . '

'Ah yes, the drive,' Gilmore interrupted smoothly. 'I wanted to ask your father about that. Do you think he'd let me come along?'

'I . . . I . . . guess you better ask him,' Maddy stammered, unable to quite believe her ears.

       ⋆   ⋆   ⋆

Wheeler and his companion reached the Flying F ranch house just after midnight and, anxious to disturb no one, they simply spread their blankets in the horse barn, having first taken care of their mounts.

Wheeler woke with the sun and cowboy-like went in search of coffee.

He was enjoying his second cup, in company with the Flying F's resident grub spoiler, one Faro Harrison, when Faulkener himself stomped into the kitchen.

Harrison, who knew his esteemed boss's moods as well as any wife, took one look at the other's face, saw the storm clouds and set mug and coffee on the table without a word.

'Damn glad to see you back, Cord,' Faulkener began, after sampling the scalding brew. 'We've had some trouble here.'

'What kind?' Wheeler asked curiously.

'Well, to start with, young Brad got careless in the horse corral yesterday and that goddamn bay devil stove him up pretty bad.

'He's OK,' the older man went on, 'but it leaves us a man short.

'And if that ain't enough, that blasted

fancy pants fiancé o' Maddy's says he wants to string along on the drive. Something about wantin' to publish a book of photographs about the West.'

'Tell him no,' Wheeler offered simply, carefully examining this new and somewhat peculiar development.

'How the hell can I?' Faulkener stormed. 'They're talkin' about gettin' married when we hit Videlio!'

'They are?' Wheeler asked gently, seeing Travis Bregan in the doorway. 'Or he is?'

'Hell, Cord, I don't know! Personally, I'd sooner see her married to a Gila monster.'

'Or an Apache?' Wheeler asked slyly.

'I killed a lot of Apache in my time,' came the crisp retort, 'but I never met one that wasn't a man, what the Mexicans call *hombre* and I never met one that made my skin crawl. An' I sure can't say that about Hank's boy.'

★　★　★

The big kitchen, which also served as the dining-room for the ranch hands, soon began to fill. Dixon arrived early and although alert for any sign Wheeler could detect neither shock or surprise on the foreman's face when the detective greeted him.

Breakfast over, the men congregated outside the bunkhouse, where Faulkener outlined the day's work.

'Doc says young Brad should be up and ridin' again in a week or so,' Faulkener began. 'But we ain't got time to wait so I'm figgerin' on takin' on a new hand.'

'Soon as you get through picking your string,' Faulkener went on, turning to his foreman, 'I want you to head for town and see who you can round up. There may be some trail-hand drifting through who wants to go north.'

'Sure boss,' Dixon responded, stepping back and unable to keep a small, secret smile from flitting across his face.

'Cattle are all branded and look fat and frisky, boys,' Faulkener went on, a smile breaking across his weather-worn face. 'All we got to do now is get 'em to Videlio.' He paused, waiting for the laugh to die.

'We'll pick our strings this mornin',' the rancher went on. 'And since Cord here's got the biggest job, I'm sayin' he gets first pick o' the cavvy.'

'Sure, boss,' Dixon responded immediately. 'And I got just the mount for him,' he went on, turning and throwing a quick wink at Breck Barker.

9

'Weren't it a bay that laid up young Brad?' Wheeler demanded as Barker led the big, skittish horse into the breaking corral.

'Sure,' Dixon sneered, disappointed that the character of the horse came as no surprise to his intended victim.

'If you don't like this one,' the *segundo* went on, 'we got a livery stable plug you can use. He may be a mite too young and skittish for a dude like you, though. Ain't but fourteen, fifteen years old.'

'Mebbe I'll look him over, if this one don't suit,' Wheeler replied equably, handing his gunbelt to Faulkener and swinging easily over the corral bars.

All trace of a limp had vanished as Wheeler moved quietly across the corral to the head of the big bay gelding, signalling Barker away from him.

Quietly and gently, the man from El Paso mumbled wordlessly to the big horse, calming him patiently with hands and voice.

Almost imperceptibly, the mustang relaxed and without making any sudden moves, Wheeler slowly gathered the reins and set one foot slowly in the stirrup, easing his weight up and swinging his other leg across.

He was barely settled in the saddle before the bay gave a pain enraged scream and exploded upwards.

Only a swift grab at the saddle-horn saved Wheeler from being ignominiously thrown and, for a time, all his energy was concentrated on staying aboard the enraged animal. Gradually, however, he managed to drag the mustang's head up, although his arms seemed to be tearing from their sockets with the strain.

Suddenly, finding himself unable to buck, the mustang began to run, kicking and jerking, trying to dislodge the hated thing on his back. But

Wheeler's iron grip on the reins never faltered and it was the pony who gave up first, ploughing to a leg-straddled, chest-heaving halt, although even in his exhausted state he was still trying to reach back and bite at the rider so firmly planted that he seemed to grow from the saddle.

Aware that there was something wrong, Wheeler was out of the saddle, almost as soon as the big horse had come to a halt, deftly avoiding the snap of the big teeth and swiftly stripping off saddle and blanket.

Under the blanket and deeply embedded in the bay's skin were a dozen choya spines, the long, poisonous needles of a common south-western cactus.

With Bregan holding the now exhausted bay's head, Wheeler gently extracted the vicious spines and, holding them in his hand, turned towards Breck Barker.

'Know what these are?' Wheeler asked mildly.

'Sure,' Barker shrugged, and the look of puzzlement on his face seemed genuine as he went on, 'but I never . . . '

That was as far as he got, because in one smooth movement, Wheeler dropped the spines in the dust and smashed his fist accurately into Barker's mouth.

The man shot backwards into the dust, to lay glaring up at Wheeler.

For a moment, neither spoke. Then Barker demanded through badly smashed lips, 'What in hell d'you do that for?'

'Well, it may come as a surprise to a rat like you,' Wheeler began icily, 'but horses ain't got much use for choya spines in their saddle blankets.'

'But . . . but . . . but, hell, I wouldn't never do that to a horse,' Barker mumbled, pausing only to spit a mouthful of blood.

'You saddled him!' Wheeler snapped accusingly.

'The damn horse was saddled when I found him!' Barker responded heatedly.

★   ★   ★

'And I believe him,' Wheeler admitted quietly to Faulkener, watching Dixon ride away towards Cartuna as the trail-hands headed for the big kitchen, having finished examining and in some cases, attending to the string of ponies assigned to them for the duration of the drive.

'But if Barker didn't,' Faulkener asked reasonably, 'who did?'

Faulkener might have gone some way towards answering his own question if he had seen the direction Dixon took once he was out of sight of the ranch buildings.

Risking a quick look over his shoulder and finding no one in sight, Dixon dragged his pony off of the main trail and headed up a barely discernible track, which led at an angle away from the main route. Ignoring his mounting fatigue, he pushed the animal mercilessly through the darkness until, with dawn still some hours away, he pulled his lathered mount to a halt on the brow of a low hill.

Swiftly unsaddling, Dixon built a

small, economical fire before rolling up in his blankets next to it. Dawn found him awake and crouched over his fire, blanket in hand and pile of green trash beginning to choke the flames.

The column of smoke thus produced rose pencil straight in the clear dawn and, within minutes, Dixon saw a similar line of smoke rising from the vicinity of the trail to Snake Pass.

Abruptly, Dixon jerked his blanket across the smouldering fire, expertly sending three long puffs into the still air. His signal sent, Dixon immediately extinguished his fire, scattering the ashes beyond hope of discovery.

The answer to his signal wasn't long in coming.

The Flying F *segundo* rode up to the ranch buildings late in the afternoon of the following day, having come back by way of town, and Faulkener had hailed him from the corral rails with the obvious question.

'Ain't just sure, Boss,' Dixon offered, with a deprecatory shrug in answer to his employer's enquiry. 'I saw a coupla likely fellas in town, told 'em to head out this way.'

'We sure got to have at least one more rider,' Faulkener grumbled. 'Could use two, really, what with young Brad bein' laid up.'

'Don't you worry, boss,' Dixon responded. 'You can bet the right man'll show up.'

'Hope you're right,' Faulkener grumbled, turning abruptly and making his way up to the house.

'You bet I'm right,' Dixon grated at his employer's slowly receding back. 'Only he'll be the right man for me . . . not you!'

★ ★ ★

It was an almost insignificant scratching at the door of his run down shack, late that night, that brought Dixon to his feet, Colt in hand.

Swiftly, he turned the lamp down to a bare glimmer, before silently easing the door open. A black shadow slipped through at floor level and having resecured the door, Dixon turned to find himself facing the shadowy form of a man with the glint of a pistol in his right hand.

'What in hell's this, Lou?' Dixon demanded.

'Just bein' careful,' the other responded, sliding away his weapon. 'Can't never be sure what's waitin' for you in the dark, Wade. No,' Dixon's visitor continued, 'leave the light. We can see well enough for what we gotta say.'

'So that's how it is, Lou.' Dixon finished, with a composure he was far from feeling. 'Gilmore gets the ranch and the girl and we get a coupla hundred dollars apiece.'

'Well, I can tell you,' the other began, 'I don't see why it has to be that way. We take all the risk rustlin' Flying F stock while fancy pants sits in his office rakin' in the chips? That don't set right with me, don't set right at all.'

Dixon, who had angled his story in the expectation of just such a reaction, grinned into the darkness.

'But what can we do, Lou?' he began with a shrug. 'If something happened to Faulkener and mebbe the kids and we had money, well, we could buy the ranch ourselves and then Gilmore'd have to let us in on his l'il game. As it is . . .'

'Mebbe that ain't such a bad notion,' the one called Lou interrupted. 'A bullet apiece'll fix the old man an' the kids,' he went on callously. 'And as for the money . . . why, we'll do her the way old man Faulkener fixed to!'

'How's that, Lou?' Dixon asked stupidly, although he guessed that his visitor was just about to sketch exactly the plan which had occurred to his own agile, vicious brain.

'Why the cows o' course, stupid,' the other snapped impatiently, fully justifying Dixon's faith in him.

'Listen,' he began swiftly. 'The buyer in Videlio don't know the old man, does he?'

'Nope,' Dixon admitted.

'Then it's easy. Listen. About three days' drive from Videlio the trail goes through a kinda ravine. Its narrow and any crew driving cows through there are gonna have their hands full. Too full to be lookin' out for trouble. So here's what we do . . . '

*　*　*

With his visitor gone the way he had come, Dixon turned the lamp back up and having opened the window to let out the smell of horse, whiskey and stale sweat that the man had brought with him, the Flying F *segundo* lounged back in the room's only comfortable chair and indulged himself in a vicious grin.

'Pie like mother made,' he congratulated himself. 'An' I do believe ol' Lou is just stupid enough to believe we'll be goin' fifty-fifty.'

'Poor ol' Lou,' Dixon commiserated with himself. 'I'll have to explain to him that a bullet is some cheaper.'

And in the shadows thrown by the adobe walls of the dusty little horse corral, now empty of stock with the coming drive, Cord Wheeler eased himself erect and made his silent way over the wall of the corral farthest from Dixon's shack.

He had moved noiselessly into the entrance of the tiny enclosure soon after full dark and laid patiently waiting, watching the door of the foreman's shack on the chance that Dixon might have just such a caller as this and although he had decided against taking the chance of eavesdropping on the pair, the visit alone told him most of what he wanted to know.

'I'd bet a stack we'll have us a visitor in the morning,' Wheeler informed himself as he approached the horse barn which contained the bay mustang and his meagre bedroll. 'An' it'll just so happen that he'll be a cow-person, fresh out of a job an' lookin' for work.'

Suddenly, in the shadow of the big

barn door something moved and instantly Wheeler dropped flat, drawing the deadly little blade from where she lived in her sheath strapped to the detective's scarred forearm. She had no name, this perfectly balanced, razor-sharp sliver of Toledo steel, but Wheeler always thought of her as "she'. In his service, she had taken many lives.

'*Quien ess Tio?*' came in a sibilant whisper from the shadows and Wheeler relaxed, recognizing Travis Bregan's voice and the accompanying *Tio*, the Spanish word for 'uncle', which signalled that the boy was alone and that his response was not being forced from him.

'*Tio* Wheeler,' the detective responded without moving. He waited for a full count of five then came silently to his feet and moved towards the barn door, all in one stealthy, cat-swift movement, sheathing the deadly little blade as he did so.

Bregan was waiting in the deeper darkness beside the barn door and it wasn't until Wheeler moved into the building against the moonlight that he holstered his battered, short barrelled Colt and said carefully, 'You were right, Cord.'

'Happens sometimes,' the man from El Paso admitted. 'So tell me about it.'

' . . . then Dixon took the short way to town and the *hombre* he was signalling to come riding down the trail from Snake Pass as if he was out for a mornin' constitutional,' Travis finished.

'Did you try back-trackin' him?' Wheeler asked with a grin.

'Sure,' the boy admitted readily. 'Found where he'd made the signal fire, 'bout halfway to the pass. From the number of empty tomato cans, he'd been there a while and it weren't the first time he'd used the place, neither.'

'Whoever he is,' Bregan went on, 'he ain't stupid. I tried to track him from the place where he'd laid the signal fire but he'd ridden around some and covered his tracks good. Tell you one thing, though,' the boy finished, hawking and spitting from a dust-filled throat. 'He didn't come from Videlio.'

'Well,' Wheeler offered, reaching down and tendering a canteen, before deftly unrolling his blankets, 'mebbe he'll tell us a bit more about hisself tomorrow.'

'What in hell . . . ' Bregan began.

'Well, he sure as hell ain't ridden all this way for the pleasure of Dixon's company,' came the acid reply.

'Nope,' Wheeler went on, scooping a hollow for his hip before rolling expertly into his blankets, 'I'm figgerin' we'll have us a visitor come sunup.'

10

As it turned out, for once, Wheeler was wrong. The Flying F received two visitors the next day, the first arriving in a hired buggy loaded with portmanteaus and a mountain of complex and delicate photographic equipment, in the person of Milton Gilmore, attorney-at-law and self-styled fiancé to Madelaine Faulkener.

'An' you can take it from me,' Faulkener growled, 'that he's about as welcome as Texas fever!'

'That ain't no way to talk about your daughter's intended,' Wheeler reproved with a broad grin. Faulkener's reply was unprintable and as it happened, anatomically extremely difficult to accomplish, but when he'd stopped for want of breath and subject matter, the old man suddenly grinned.

'Hell, Cord,' he said quickly, nudging

the man from El Paso. 'Look at young Travis. Ain't he a picture! Makes you glad you ain't their age, don't it?'

'Sure,' Wheeler smiled, easing down from the corral rail he had been sharing with his employer. 'But I guess I'll mebbe give him a hand.'

Wheeler was barely halfway to the toiling group, however, when a grinning Charlie Faulkener, on the other end of a bulky portmanteau from a scowling Travis Bregan, suddenly dropped his end of their burden and pushed, depositing Bregan, who had been glaring in the direction of Gilmore and his intended, into the dust, with the portmanteau on top of him.

'You Goddamn dirty 'breed . . . ' Gilmore screamed womanishly as, forgetful of Maddy Faulkener, he hurled himself around the half-empty buggy. There was, however, nothing womanish about the quirt-filled hand he drew back to slash across the younger man's unprotected face.

Only his Indian speed saved Bregan

as he twisted aside, barely dodging the first blow and struggling to free himself of the heavy trunk. Desperately, he thrust the encumbering thing aside, driving to his feet and grabbing at his pistol, which chose this moment to jam solidly in its battered old holster.

Luckily for him, there was no need for a weapon, because even as Gilmore drew back his arm for a second blow Wheeler had covered the distance separating him from the attorney and driven the heel of his moccasin savagely in behind Gilmore's knee.

Unable to maintain his balance, the lawyer pitched forward, landing on his knees and positioning himself perfectly for Wheeler's fist, which slammed into the base of his skull in a beautifully executed rabbit punch. Without a sound, Gilmore folded into the dirt.

'You better let me look at that holster before you're much older, Travis,' Wheeler ordered softly, hauling the younger man to his feet, 'on account of there's some of us sure figger on you gettin' a lot older,' he finished whimsically pointing to where a white-faced Maddy Faulkener was looking anxiously in his direction.

Seeing Travis's unabashed grin, she tossed her head and flounced away. Unfortunately, she forget to look where she was going and measured her length in the dust of the yard and to add insult to injury it was Travis who reached her first, just as Dixon's overnight visitor pulled his jaded horse to a halt in front of the bunkhouse.

★　★　★

'Name's Robles, Lou Robles,' the cowboy offered shortly, after the dust had settled and Maddy had conducted a furious Gilmore into the ranch house. 'Your man here,' he went on, jerking a thumb in Dixon's direction, 'said you was hirin'.'

'Sure,' Faulkener admitted, observing as he spoke that Robles's gear was all of the right quality for a topgrade cowhand and that his hands showed the heavy calluses a man only gets from constant rope work.

'All right,' the old rancher went on abruptly, 'I pay $40 a month and keep. We're driving in the morning, so pick your string from what's left. Sleep in the bunkhouse tonight. My boys are night-herding so we can start fresh in the morning. See my foreman,' he indicated Dixon, 'about anything else.'

'OK . . . Boss,' the pause was barely long enough to be insulting, but only barely. As Robles turned away, he caught Dixon's eye and Wheeler, who had been watching for it, saw the conspiratorial look that passed between the two men.

* * *

'Whew, she was mad,' Travis admitted miserably to a preoccupied Cord Wheeler the next day, as they scouted the route some miles ahead of the main body of the herd which Faulkener, who was his own trail boss, had started from the bedding ground, on the well-marked trail to Videlio, well before first light.

'She said Gilmore was tagging along 'cause they was gonna get married in Videlio and he's got some idea about photographin' a cattle drive and bein' famous. She sure seems set, Cord,' the boy finished disconsolately.

'Don't bet on it,' Wheeler offered thoughtfully. 'I wonder why he's so interested in Miz Maddy, though.'

'Why just 'cause she's beautiful and when she smiles . . . ' Bregan began.

'Not enough for a man like Gilmore,' Wheeler interrupted.

'Watch the trail,' he ordered suddenly, abruptly wheeling the bay. 'I got to ask Faulkener a question.'

★   ★   ★

'How did you guess about the rustling?' the old man demanded, after Wheeler had found him and put his question.

129

'Just figgered it was possible,' Wheeler said simply. 'It made sense of some of the other things that have happened.'

'Well, we ain't been losin' that many,' Faulkener admittedl. 'Just enough to make me sore.'

'And about enough to keep a gang o' men in wages 'til somethin' better turned up?' Wheeler wondered out loud.

'Mebbe,' the old man admitted. 'What you thinkin' Cord?'

'I'm thinkin' mebbe the snake I'm after is a sight more poisonous than I thought,' came the laconic answer.

Suddenly, a steer ducked and backed out of the herd clearly intent upon freedom, but a hard-riding Charlie Faulkener on a nimble little roan, turned the errant beast forcing it reluctantly back into the herd.

'I reckon Charlie's the oldest out of him and Miz Maddy,' Wheeler asked absently.

'Certainly,' Faulkener agreed, 'though he doesn't always act it!'

'He'll settle down,' Wheeler offered

gravely although, for once, his cold green eyes were warmed by a smile. 'Most of us do.'

'So I'm guessin' he stands to inherit, if . . . ' Wheeler paused awkwardly.

'If I put my checks back in the rack, you mean?' Faulkener finished for him bluntly.

'Sure,' Wheeler agreed, 'though I'm guessin' that'll be a while.'

'You'd mebbe guess wrong!' Faulkener snapped abruptly and when Wheeler looked his question, the old man went on.

'Weren't feelin' so well coupla months back so I went to see Hank. Told me my heart wasn't as good as it could be.'

'Ha!' Faulkener barked, plainly goaded by the memory. 'He told me to take it easy! As if I can take it easy with this damn spread to run!'

'Don't get me wrong, Cord,' Faulkener went on quickly. 'My Charlie's a good boy but he's still young and full of sass. Needs someone to help him and, between you and me, I ain't sure Wade's quite the man for the job.'

'I'd say you called that about right,' Wheeler agreed. 'Anyone else know about your ticker?'

'Well, I didn't want the kids havin' any trouble if something did happen to me so I made a will. Had it notarized in town.'

'And let me guess,' Wheeler suggested acidly, 'Milt Gilmore did the work for you?'

'Sure not hard to guess that,' Faulkener bridled. 'Seeing as how he's the only lawyer in the place.'

'And how long after that did he come courtin' Miz Maddy?' Wheeler asked mildly.

For a long moment Faulkener glared at the man from El Paso.

'Cord,' the old man began eventually, 'that ain't a very pretty picture you're paintin'.'

'I'm hopin' it don't get no uglier,' came the blunt response.

★　★　★

'Why in hell you loafin' here?' Wheeler demanded, as he eased back to ride beside Travis Bregan, who had dropped so far behind the herd that the curses of the riders herding the drag were only a faint echo.

'Waitin for you,' came the instant retort.

'Don't look round,' Bregan went on, before Wheeler could respond. 'We've got some company.'

'Who?' Wheeler asked softly.

'Ain't sure,' Travis admitted. 'Seen a flash from a gun barrel or mebbe field glasses coupla hours ago. Spotted them a coupla times since. There's sure more than one but can't tell no more.'

'Probably friends of Mr Robles and likely in the same line of business,' Wheeler offered.

'What business?' Travis demanded.

'The cow business, leastwise, as long as they're somebody else's cows,' Wheeler began whimsically, before going on to give Bregan a brief account of his morning's conversation with Faulkener.

'How'd you figger he's a rustler?' Bregan demanded.

'When he rode in yesterday, he left that pony of his at the hitching rail,' Wheeler began.

'So?' the other demanded.

'Never tied him. Just draped the rein over the rail,' Wheeler explained. 'Ain't but one sort of feller takes the time to teach his pony a trick like that, and that's a feller who may need his pony in a hurry. Like an outlaw.'

'And you figger Robles has got friends along?' Travis asked after he had digested Wheeler's explanation.

'We'll know tonight,' Wheeler stated. 'After you an' me take a look at them.'

* * *

'Looks real peaceful, don't it?' Wheeler offered as he and Travis lay amongst a small stand of live oaks, looking down on a low-lying stretch of sand, where three blanket-wrapped shapes lay huddled round a dwindling fire.

The detective and his young companion had slipped away from the herd as soon as the moon had risen and guided by the faint glow from the bandit's fire, they had easily found the camp site.

'Sure lucky for us, when you come to think about it,' Wheeler mused. 'Them fellers build a nice big fire to guide us to where they're at and then, just about the coldest part of the night, they let it go out. And they don't leave no one on guard,' he finished, pointing to where three hobbled horses stamped and fidgeted.

'Stay here,' Wheeler ordered his companion abruptly. 'I think I'll take a l'il look around.' And before Travis could open his mouth, his companion was gone.

Seconds dragged into minutes, while Travis waited behind the big boulder which he and Wheeler had selected as a vantage point.

Without warning, there came the scrape of boot heel striking stone and

Travis twisted like a cat, clawing at his pistol, because Wheeler wore no boots, instead opting for the knee-high Apache moccasins that Dallas Bregan had made for him.

'Uh, uh, uh *amigo*,' came a sneering Mexican voice, high and to the left, although search as he might, Bregan could find no sign of its owner.

'Get rid of *la pistola, amigo*,' the voice ordered oilily and, when Travis had complied, he heard a scraping followed by a series of dry clicks before a swarthy, thick-set Mexican waddled into sight, clutching a battered Colt.

Carefully, Travis raised his hands, mind and body strung to readiness for what he knew would have to be a desperate gamble. If ever they got him down to the fire . . .

'*Saludos, amigo*,' Bregan began. 'I was lost and saw your fire . . . '

'It is not nice to lie to someone you have only just met, gringo,' the Mexican interrupted. 'You are with the trail herd. My *amigos* and I have been

136

watching you all of today. We thought mebbe a gringo would be stupid enough to come lookin' for us if he saw a fire. An' wha' do you know. Look, that's just wha' happened.'

11

Without taking his eyes from his prisoner the swarthy Mexican cupped a hand around his mouth.

'Rauol, Esteban,' he bellowed. 'Come see what I have fou . . . '

But his last word died in a horrible gurgle as he jerked forwards, pawing at his throat, from where the ivory handle of a throwing knife suddenly seemed to be growing.

Without a sound, Wheeler slipped around the trunk of the stunted oak where he had stood concealed and jerked the knife out of his still-twitching victim.

'Get your Colt,' he snapped at a shocked Travis Bregan, as he rolled the body into a convenient crevice and began to scatter twigs and other debris over it. 'And don't waste no time. Them boys'll be lookin' for their *amigo* and

138

we sure better be long gone afore they find him.'

★   ★   ★

Dawn had come and the herd was moving steadily forward, settling now into a routine with most of the steers occupying the places they would travel in for the whole of the journey, before Wheeler and Bregan managed to catch up.

Bregan had been uncommunicative during the ride back and as his companion swung down, preparatory to changing his mount he demanded, 'You set me up, didn't you, Cord?'

'Nope,' the other returned. 'Had no choice. I heard our deceased and unlamented friend movin' about back o' the trees and I didn't have no time to do anything but slip out. Barely got round behind him before he opened his mouth. If it helps, I'm sorry. Next times I'll be the pigeon but afore you say anything else, we got other things to think about.

'We'll hit Snake Pass today,' Wheeler went on. 'She's a dandy place for an ambush or other such foolishness. So you stick closer to Miz Maddy than a tick on a dog.'

'What about you?' Travis asked.

'Oh, I'll be around,' Wheeler stated flatly and, with that, the young man had to be content.

★ ★ ★

Late morning sun slanted down on the herd as Blue Dogie, the giant lead bull of the Flying F, breasted the gently sloping trail that led up to the pass, giving vent to a mournful bellow as he did so, almost as though he were warning his companions of the tribulations which lay just ahead.

'Keep 'em moving boys,' Faulkener roared, urging his horse up the shallow grade. 'We gotta get 'em through before dark, or Christ knows what'll happen,' he finished, as, urged on by the yelling drovers, the main body of the herd moved reluctantly up towards the entrance to the pass.

'We'll make Jacob's Eddy by tonight,' Charlie Falkener yelled at Cord Wheeler, who was riding next to him. Wheeler nodded, ignoring the labouring cattle and continuing to scan the outcrops and ledges of the rock-bound pass the herd was entering.

Hours crept by and the leading steers had just reached the highest point of the trail and begun the gradual descent to the flat desert lands below when, from high amongst the rocks that overlooked the narrowest section of the pass, which the main body of the herd was jostling its way through, a fusillade of shots rang out.

Instantly, almost as one beast, the panicked herd tried to run, several of the weaker animals falling to be trampled underfoot as the cursing cowboys tried to avoid the flailing death that surrounded them.

Wheeler, pushing carefully to the edge of the herd on a big raw-boned chestnut that seemed to relish the job, had just caught sight of Charlie Faulkener a little ahead of him, when Faulkener's horse appeared to stagger, before pitching sideways into the struggling mass of bodies.

Although it seemed certain that the boy must have been torn to ribbons, Wheeler nevertheless began to force his mount through the press of steers to be suddenly rewarded by the sight of Faulkener clinging precariously to a spur of rock which, with incredible luck, had been within snatching distance when his pony went down.

'Hang on,' Wheeler bellowed unnecessarily, spurring his labouring pony towards the near-vertical rock wall.

He was almost within reach of the boy when suddenly the spur cracked and gave way, depositing Faulkener in the path of a maddened steer.

But before the boy's feet had touched the ground Wheeler's pistol was in his hand and bellowing, as fast as the detective could work the trigger.

Shot neatly in the back of the head, the steer immediately threatening the youngster dropped in its tracks, to be followed almost instantly by four more, their bodies forming a low barricade in front of Faulkener.

For an instant the obstacle checked the steers beyond it and in that split second of time, Wheeler had forced his mount to the boy's side and jerked him up and across the saddle.

Instantly, Wheeler spurred the chestnut and the big horse responded gallantly, shouldering his way through the now thinning press of frightened beasts and making for a wider section of the trail up ahead where the herd was spreading out and slowing its terror-stricken run.

But even as the big mustang forced its way out of the herd, a nearby steer, eyes rolling with fright, hooked backwards and slashed the razor-sharp tip of its horn across the flank of Wheeler's mount. Driven mad with pain, the pony bucked sideways, all but throwing Wheeler and his burden from the saddle.

Desperately, Wheeler dragged on the reins, forcing the horse's head up as the big animal snorted and bucked in its pain and fear and gradually, as the pain subsided, Wheeler regained control and was able to begin forcing his way out of the now exhausted herd.

★   ★   ★

'Jesus, Cord,' Charlie Faulkener began shakily as, once arrived at bed ground just outside the exit from the pass, Wheeler had helped him down. 'I sure wish I could find me a high-stake poker game tonight. My luck sure must be in.'

'I'm thankin' you,' the boy went on shyly, extending his hand before Wheeler could answer.

'Hell, don't mention nothin' about that,' Wheeler shrugged, shaking quickly to hide his embarrassment. 'Mebbe best though you don't say nothin' about this,' he added thoughtfully.

'Sure, Cord, whatever you say is sure

good enough for me,' the puzzled boy agreed.

* * *

'Could've been worse,' Faulkener admitted, when Wheeler caught up with him. 'Leastways looks like everybody's alive.'

'I wouldn't be so sure of that, boss,' Dixon interrupted, riding up on the rancher's near side. 'Breck says he ain't seen Sol since the herd started running.'

* * *

It was the pitiful whinnying of a horse in pain that led Wheeler to the spot and it didn't need more than one look to confirm that Sol Barker was beyond any help in this life.

Abruptly, Wheeler jerked out his pistol and fired three rapid shots into Barker's stricken mount, ending its suffering as he simultaneously gave the rangeland's universal plea for help.

Breck Barker was the first to arrive and Wheeler swung his tired pony in front of the big man.

'You don't want to look at him,' Wheeler said tiredly. 'You sure can't do him no good at all.'

Wordlessly, Barker kneed his pony past the detective, as the rest of the crew approached. Moments later, Wheeler heard the sounds of vomiting from the place where what was left of Sol Barker lay.

'You sure it's Sol?' an ashen-faced Charlie Faulkener demanded, looking down at what remained of his friend.

'Well, he was wearin' a calico shirt just like that one,' Dixon responded, callously poking at the shredded cloth with his foot. 'And there sure ain't no one else missin'.'

'Sure, couldn't tell who it was no other way,' Robles offered with a sneering laugh. 'Still,' he went on, 'we won't need no tarp to wrap him in. Best just pour him into the hole.'

Before anyone else could respond to this callous suggestion, Breck Barker had twisted clumsily and slammed a meaty fist in to the side of Robles's head.

The big drover staggered and dropped to a knee instinctively palming his pistol and causing Barker to halt in his tracks.

'I'm gonna kill you for that, you stupid bas — ' Robles began, lifting his Colt.

'No, you ain't,' a cold voice assured him and Robles kept very still, because the voice was accompanied by the muzzle of a pistol, which had come to rest just under his left ear.

'Drop it,' the voice ordered and then Robles was jerked abruptly to his feet.

Turning, he found himself facing a cold-eyed Cord Wheeler, the long-barrelled Smith and Wesson now back in its holster.

'You're a funny man,' Wheeler said gently. 'I hope you don't end up bein' too funny for your own good. You want any more of him, Mr Barker?' he went on, looking past the incensed Robles.

'No,' the big man answered brokenly. 'I . . . I . . . '

'We'll take care of Sol for you, Breck,' Charlie Faulkener assured the big man, coming forward with a tarp and carefully laying it over Barker's remains.

'A couple of you boys get some shovels and you and me'll pick him out a good spot, Breck,' the boy went on, taking the big man by the arm and gently leading him away.

'I'll take my gun now,' Robles snarled, stooping to retrieve the weapon, only to freeze into stillness as Wheeler spoke.

'Sure and if you figure to use it, why, go ahead. You sure ain't never gonna get a better chance.'

For one tense instant, it seemed as if Robles might answer his tormentor with gunplay, but something about the slim figure before him, its thumb hooked in the broad, cartridge-studded gunbelt next to the worn butt of the Smith and Wesson seemed to give him pause.

Then the instant had passed and Robles was easing carefully erect, the butt of his pistol grasped between thumb and forefinger, plainly and unmistakably intent upon no hostile move.

'You'll keep, Fancy Pants,' the drover sneered as he eased his gun carefully back into its holster.

'Sure,' Wheeler agreed with an easy shrug, then his left hand blurred, slapping Robles hard across the mouth.

Involuntarily the drover's hand jerked gunwards only to freeze instantly as he found the muzzle of Wheeler's pistol boring into his belly.

'I don't usually give snakes a second chance,' Wheeler softly informed the now terrified Robles. 'Next time you try and pull on me you may find yourself a touch late. As in 'the late Mr Robles',' the man from El Paso finished with a hard grin.

★   ★   ★

'Sure looks like it weren't no accident,' Wheeler informed himself, looking down at the body of the little sorrel

149

which had so nearly been the death of Charlie Faulkener.

Taking advantage of the arrangements associated with Barker's funeral, Wheeler had slipped away from camp an hour before dusk, to examine the body and it had been the work of a moment to determine that the little pony had been shot.

'Bullet went in the right side,' Wheeler mused. 'Just under the heart. Pistol by the size of it. An' the way Charlie was facing, it couldn't have been done by one of the fellas who started the stampede. Which leaves . . . '

★   ★   ★

Later that night, as he sat on his bedroll, finishing his fifth cup of the brew that Faulkener's cook passed off as coffee, Wheeler examined the remaining group of twelve men scattered around the dying embers of the cook fire.

Dixon, the remaining Barker and Robles sat in a huddled, whispering group to one side, Barker and Robles apparently having buried their differences.

The rest, which consisted of Faulkener, his son Charlie, Gilmore, three of Faulkener's ranch-bands, all that could be spared from the routine ranch work and four new hands, taken on for the duration of the drive, lay sprawled disconsolately around the fire, most still eating the substantial stew which was the trail driver's staple diet. Maddy Faulkener had already retired to her bedroll in the chuck wagon.

Mentally, Wheeler ticked off their relative positions during that day's work. Dixon and Barker had ridden point, the front of the herd, while Faulkener had assigned the four new men to the rear or drag along with two of his own men, all too far away to have done the shooting. Which left at least Robles unaccounted for.

Finding he could get no further Wheeler moved over next to Faulkener and after a few moments' conversation,

151

put his question.

'Opposite you and Charlie?' Faulkener repeated. 'Hard to say,' the old rancher admitted. 'We was so mixed up it could have been anyone.'

And with that answer Wheeler had to be content.

12

'Sure looks peaceful, don't it?' Travis Bregan observed, gazing down at the long stream of fat contented steers wending their way lazily towards the distant horizon.

'Sure does,' his companion, Maddy Faulkener, agreed. 'Dad was real pleased to get through the desert without losing any. He said if you hadn't been so clever at finding water, we'd have lost quite a few.'

The herd had been on the trail now for all of two months and, with what the crew hoped was the worst part of the trip over, Bregan and Maddy were finding themselves increasingly thrown together.

'Oh,' the boy prevaricated, 'that weren't me. Cord done most of the work. Anyhow,' Bregan went on, quickly changing the subject 'shouldn't be no more problems with water. Yonder's the Mescal,' he explained, pointing to the barely discernible silver ribbon, showing just below the distant horizon.

'She's pretty deep in places,' he observed, trying to ignore the girl's smiling eyes, 'so we'll have to swim the herd. Once we're through that, though, it's only about ten days to Videlio, on an easy trail. And then we'll all be dancing at your wedding,' he finished miserably.

'I guess so,' the girl admitted, although without any show of enthusiasm.

In truth, she was beginning to have very serious doubts about Gilmore, the man who had seemed so eligible back in Cartuna.

His vicious attack on Travis over something as unimportant as a dropped trunk had shaken her to the core and on the trip north he hadn't shown to advantage, spending his days on the seat of the chuck wagon, endlessly rehearsing a list of complaints which grew longer with each new day on the trail. His complaining had only ceased on those rare occasions when he had dragged his camera from the back of the wagon and taken a few desultory pictures.

'How long before we hit your old river?' she teased, glad to be in Bregan's company and resolutely forcing the subject of her self-proclaimed fiancé to the back of her mind.

'Oh, couple days should see us there,' the other answered, flashing a rare smile that Maddy was finding had the surprising ability to make her heart skip.

*   *   *

'She looks pretty high, Drew,' Wheeler observed, as two days later, he and Faulkener sat their ponies on a low bluff overlooking the flat, sloping banks of the Mescal.

'Hell, once we get him started across, ol' Dogie'll just naturally drag that bunch along behind him, horns, hide and taller,' Faulkener assured him.

'I'm believin' you,' Wheeler admitted, squinting knowledgeably at the sun. 'Bed 'em down here. I'm gonna give that little bit of a stream a try.'

The streambed proved to be rock and hard, firm sand after Wheeler had urged his canny bay into the water, its bed shelving quickly, to bring the water up to the pony's knees.

Wheeler pushed on steadily, finding only a single narrow stretch of swimming water in the middle of the river and reaching the opposite bank without further incident.

With his clothes drying rapidly in the late afternoon sun, Wheeler urged the willing bay up the slope, examining the state of the shore as he did so.

'Looks as good a place as any,' Wheeler informed his pony, turning the big horse back towards the stream and letting him take his own time about the crossing.

The return journey was accomplished

as easily as the first trip and arriving safely on the other bank, Wheeler turned in his saddle.

'Looks like this should be pie like mother made, old horse,' he offered, thereby tempting Fate, who must have decided that Wheeler had had more than his fair share of luck already.

*   *   *

'Now what in hell is that idiot Gilmore doin'?' Wheeler demanded caustically of no one in particular as, next morning, with the sun barely showing through a cloud-topped horizon, he watched Cartuna's most eminent lawyer and Maddy Faulkener's only fiancé fiddling with some very expensive-looking photographic equipment.

'Mornin' Mr Gilmore,' Wheeler offered blandly, riding up to where the man had mounted his equipment on the low bluff from where Faulkener and Wheeler had surveyed the river only the day before. Gilmore glared back at the detective.

The pair had barely spoken since Wheeler had prevented the attorney's assault on Travis Bregan and Gilmore felt something should be said to redress the balance.

'What d'you want, Mr Wheeler?' he snapped feeling, like Napoleon, that the best defence was attack.

'If you're contemplating another unprovoked assault on me, you better think again!' Gilmore went on, before the other could reply. 'And don't think you've heard the last of that other business. You may well find yourself in court before long.'

'Be pleased to see you there, Mr Gilmore,' Wheeler responded affably, the unholy light of mischief twinkling in his cold, green eyes. 'An' I'm sure the good folks of Cartuna'll be glad to hear how you took after an unarmed kid with a quirt. Especially when he was lyin' under one of your trunks at the time and couldn't defend hisself.'

Before Gilmore could reply, a worried-looking Dale Faulkener appeared at Wheeler's elbow.

'It's raining up country,' he began without preamble, pointing towards the low range of hills with their crown of dark clouds, into which the Mescal meandered.

'If we don't get across before noon,' the old man went on, 'we could be here for days and this ain't perzactly the place I'd choose to graze a herd on.'

'I'll get the boys,' Wheeler returned and, tickling the bay with spurs, he rocketed towards the camp.

★   ★   ★

'Just let 'em drift in easy, boys,' Faulkener roared as, urged on by their leather-lunged protectors, the first steers followed Blue Dogie into the icy water.

'Can't rush 'em too much, Cord,' Faulkener offered worriedly, as he watched a random branch, still in leaf, collide with one of the labouring animals. 'But we daren't take too long. Looks like that upcountry rain is pretty bad.'

'Sure,' Wheeler agreed. 'If it's pushing live trees like that one over, you can figger we're in for it if we don't rush them steers across. And she's risin' fast. Them cows are swimming already,' he finished, pointing to where Maddy Faulkener was urging a group of recalcitrant beasts across the river.

'I sure wish that gal'd stay with the wagon. She's just like her m — '

But almost before the words had left the old rancher's mouth, there was an intense flash of light from the bluff where Gilmore had set up his camera and almost as one animal the remainder of the herd, which up until then had been in hand and making the crossing in good order, plunged towards the sloping riverbank.

The whole drive could have finished there in a welter of drowned cattle and cowboys, except Charlie Faulkener and Travis Bregan plunged into the middle of the herd emptying their Colts into the nearest steers in an almost suicidal attempt to turn them back from the river.

For a single tense second the fate of the herd hung in the balance but with the riders in the drag adding their own yells and gunfire to the cacophony of noise, the remainder of the herd suddenly turned tail, plunging away up the bank of the river.

'Keep 'em bunched boys,' Charlie Faulkener screamed, his youthful voice cracking as it rose above the bellowing of the frightened steers and he spurred his tough little pony after the rapidly departing herd.

Travis Bregan was turning his mount to follow, when a cry from behind him brought his attention back to the river and what he saw there brought his heart into his mouth and made him send his mount plunging into the cold water.

Maddy Faulkener had been swimming her pony next to a small group of steers when the rest had stampeded. Wise in the ways of cows, she hadn't panicked, being content to keep the animals in her charge moving forward.

Unfortunately, the steer immediately downstream of her had other ideas and finding momentary purchase on the bed of the river, it had jerked sideways and plunged its needle-pointed horn into the side of Maddy Faulkener's unfortunate pony, by sheer bad luck, killing it instantly and knocking the girl from the saddle.

It was her single muffled scream that had caught Travis's attention and, without thinking, he threw himself out of the saddle as the girl swept past, grasping her under the arms and kicking desperately in a vain attempt to reach the safety of the shore.

Like Romeo and Juliet, the two lovers would have died there, except Cord Wheeler, seeing the couple's plight, forced his bay into the river and neatly dropped his rope over Travis Bregan's outstretched arm, just as the pair were disappearing below the surface of the Mescal.

Carefully, Wheeler eased the big bay backwards up the slope but, in roping the pair, Wheeler had been forced to move off the hard-packed sand of the ford and into the more fluid bed of the river. Gradually, the extra weight began to tell and despite his best efforts the bay began to slip and flounder, being dragged more deeply into the icy water as the liquid sand plucked at his legs.

'Cord, Cord,' a voice suddenly bellowed from up the slope and Wheeler looked up to find Charlie Faulkener waving a rope.

'Get downstream!' Wheeler urged, 'and get a rope on them two!'

Faulkener needed no further instruction and within minutes, the young rancher had neatly dabbed his loop over the pair. A waved sombrero informed the detective of that fact and it was with some relief that Wheeler dropped his lariat and began the task of extracting the fear-stricken bay from what might easily have been his sandy coffin.

It took Wheeler longer than he had expected to coax the big horse up the bank and out of the water but once standing on solid ground, a swift examination showed Wheeler that his mount had appeared to have suffered no harm from his ordeal.

'Guess I better go and separate them two wildcats,' Wheeler told the still skittish bay as he mounted and urged his pony along the bank to where he had last seen Charlie Faulkener.

★   ★   ★

'Don't you touch him, Charlie, goddamn you!'

Maddy Faulkener's voice came drifting up the trail towards him as Wheeler breasted a little hump and pulled his mount gently to a stop, looking down on the little scene before him.

Travis Bregan had been propped carefully against a convenient boulder, while in front of him displaying all the calmness and moderation of temperament one might expect from a mother leopard defending her only cub, stood Maddy Faulkener, apparently wrestling with her brother Charlie.

With a massive push Maddy hurled her brother away from her, throwing him on to his back.

'You keep away from him, Charlie Faulkener,' she snapped. 'I love him and you ain't gonna touch him!'

'Sis, that's fine with me but ... ' Faulkener began, only to stop in mid-sentence as a grinning Cord Wheeler pulled his mount to a halt next to the little group.

'Howdy, Cord,' Charlie offered. 'You got any insanity in your family?' he demanded, as a groan from a recovering Travis Bregan sent Maddy scurrying to his side.

'Nope,' Wheeler answered judiciously, after a moment's thought. 'My family usually die o' drink or cards or lead poisoning.'

'Tell you this though,' Wheeler went on. 'If your sister's chosen young Travis over Gilmore, I should say you ain't got no worries about her on that score.'

'Hell, I'm agreein' with you on that,'

Faulkener responded with a frank smiled. 'He's sure got sand. And I'm plannin' on tellin' him that as soon as that l'il spitfire Maddy lets me powwow with him.'

13

' . . . An' then he threw himself into the water after her and . . . '

'Charlie, shut up, will you?' Travis Bregan interrupted plaintively as Faulkener seemed about to launch himself into yet another account of their adventures at the river.

'But Travis, son,' the young rancher began with a wink in the direction of his father and Cord Wheeler seated on the opposite side of the fire, 'you're a forsure hero, and I'm just makin' the most of it.'

''Course,' Faulkener went on blandly, 'I ain't talkin' about you rescuin' Maddy the way you done, 'cause any of us coulda done that. No, what I mean is you aimin' to start sparkin' her. Me, I'd sooner try gettin' a calf away from a hungry cougar.'

'Huh, any girl you started sparkin' would probably choose the cougar,'

came Maddy Faulkener's sleepy voice
from under Travis Bregan's arm.

★　★　★

Chasing and rounding up the remains
of the herd on the other bank of the
Mescal had taken until nightfall and
Faulkener had decided that with the
river still rising, any crossing would
have to wait until daylight.

Since the steers which had remained
behind accounted for only about half
the herd and Faulkener, on the opposite
bank, was short-handed, Wheeler, Maddy,
Charlie and Travis had swum their ponies
across, once the river's flow had stead-
ied and made the crossing nothing more
than a matter of routine. Robles, Dixon
and two of the Flying F hands had been
left to hold the herd remaining on that
side of the Mescal, along with a disgruntled Milt Gilmore.

★　★　★

A clatter of spurs and neighing of horses announced the departure of the hands standing the first night-herd and as if it were a signal, a grey-faced Dale Faulkener stood up and stretched, before running a shaking hand across his raddled cheek.

'I'm gonna hit my blankets,' he informed nobody in particular, before turning to trudge away to where his bedroll had been placed.

One by one the rest of the crew followed suit, although it seemed to take Maddy Faulkener a peculiarly long time to arrange her blankets, despite having Bregan's able assistance.

Finally, only Wheeler remained by the fire, staring into the coals and drawing on the inevitable black cigar.

The man from El Paso had a lot to think about.

Increasingly, at the end of the day's work, Dale Faulkener had found it difficult to do more than slump into his blankets, uncharacteristically leaving Wheeler or Dixon to make the dispositions for the night-herd and deal with the hundred and one problems that nightfall invariably brought to a cattle drive.

Wheeler had shouldered the extra burden without complaint, knowing his employer to be a sick man, sicker perhaps even than Faulkener himself realized. And he wasn't alone in his concern, because more than once he had seen Maddy Faulkener glancing anxiously in her father's direction.

Tonight, however, he had seemed worse than usual and Wheeler resolved privately to try and persuade the older man to ride in the wagon for a day or two, once the herd was together and the easy part of the drive was before them.

'Sure ain't gonna be easy, though,' Wheeler admitted, grinning into the darkness. 'The old moss-head won't like sittin' back. But I guess the youngster has to start sometime and Charlie sure has got his growth on this drive.'

Having made his decision, Wheeler turned his attention to more immediate problems.

'Them critters this side'll be OK, but I'm sure figgerin' it wouldn't hurt to pay them other yahoos a li'l surprise visit before I turn in,' he decided, rising and moving towards the bay, who was picketed nearby and cropping his way steadily through the sparse forage at the end of the picket rope.

But this time, Wheeler's instincts were slow.

He had barely urged his mount into the dark water, when there came the crash of two shots from the far bank, followed by yelling and the drumming of a thousand hoofs, accompanied by a fusillade of gunfire. Behind him, Wheeler heard the rest of the herd stir restlessly, woken and made uneasy by their former companions' stampeding run.

By the time Wheeler had urged his tired mount out on the opposite bank of the Mescal, the bed ground was empty and a huddled shadow showed where at least one man had died doing his duty.

Respectfully, Wheeler turned the body on its back only to be interrupted by a voice at his shoulder.

'So they got Billy . . . ' the drover began, only to find himself suddenly looking down the bore of Wheeler's Smith and Wesson.

'Jesus, Sammy,' Wheeler swore at the terrified youngster, as he eased the hammer of his pistol. 'Don't you know better'n to sneak up on a fella. I sure mighta perforated you, you damn idjit.'

'S-s-sorry Cord,' the boy stammered. 'I sure wasn't thinkin', what with bein' shot at an' such.'

'All right, son,' Wheeler went on more gently. 'Best you try an' tell me what happened.'

* * *

'Looks like Dixon and Robles was in it together,' Wheeler explained to an enraged Charlie Faulkener, when the latter crossed the river in search of the lost herd.

'Robles and young Billy were night-herding. Seems like Robles is mebbe the boss o' that rustlin' gang your pa was so worried about before we left.'

'Anyhow,' the detective went on, 'some of his riders musta snuck up on the herd. Robles plugs Billy and Dixon takes a whang at Sammy, but misses, what with the dark and Sammy already being on the move.'

'They got the rest of the herd and we get left with one dead cow-hand to bury,' Wheeler finished.

'I'm aimin' to square up for Billy,' Faulkener snapped. 'And get them cows back!'

'Sure, I'm agreein' with you,' came the soft reply. 'But it'll do no good to go off half-cocked. We gotta figger things close. And the first thing we better do is count heads. Where's Gilmore?' the man from El Paso finished.

'I'm here,' a surly voice snapped from out of the darkness, to be accompanied moments later by a much bedraggled Milt Gilmore.

'I heard the shooting,' the lawyer began angrily, his handsome face taking on a petulant sneer. 'And since I didn't have a gun and could do no good without one, I stayed where I was.'

'D'you see which way they went?' Wheeler asked mildly, although his cold eyes missed nothing of the lawyer's demeanour.

'No, I didn't!' Gilmore snapped pettishly. 'That damn Dixon and his friend got away before I got a chance to see. When I catch up with that son of a bitch, I'll . . . '

'Get yourself killed probably,' Wheeler interrupted. 'And if you're gonna start talkin' like that, Mr Gilmore, you'd also better start carrying a gun . . . and learn how to use it,' he finished.

'When I need your goddamn advice I'll ask for it,' Gilmore snarled, right hand rising to momentarily hover near the left lapel of his dusty broadcloth jacket.

'Anyhow,' Wheeler went on, turning away and apparently not noticing the significance of the lawyer's movement, 'We got other things to think about.'

'Get your pony, Charlie,' the detective ordered. 'We'd best powwow with your dad before we decide our next move.'

More trouble was waiting on the other side of the river, however.

An ashen-faced Maddy Faulkener met the pair as Wheeler and her brother urged their ponies up the bank.

'It's Dad,' she began helplessly. 'I can't wake him.'

Faulkener lay in his blanket, his breathing shallow and uneven. A moment's examination was enough to tell Wheeler what had happened.

'He's had a stroke,' the detective said gently. 'Can't tell how bad 'til he wakes up.'

'Can we move him?' Charlie Faulkener responded quickly.

'Can or can't don't matter, Charlie,' Maddy Faulkener snapped, brushing a hand quickly across her eyes. 'We've got to and that's all there is to it. He'll die out here if'n we don't get him to the doctor in Videlio!' She turned away, this daughter of a pioneer woman, ready and more than willing to begin the fight for the father she loved.

And Wheeler hadn't the heart to tell her that it could all be pointless or that there was a good chance Faulkener might be a corpse by morning.

★　★　★

Dawn, however, found Faulkener not only breathing more easily but also awake.

'Got to get them ... cows back ... Cord,' he managed, after the situation had been explained to him. 'Got ... to ... '

'Don't worry, Dale,' Wheeler assured him. 'That's just what we aim to do.'

'Here's how I figger it,' Wheeler began crisply, rising and turning away from the man on the blanket to address the group assembled by the chuck wagon.

'Charlie, Miz Maddy and most of the crew got to push on and at least get what we got left of the herd to Videlio and your dad's buyer.' He paused, before saying softly, 'Also, you got to get your dad to a doctor. Him wakin' up so soon is about the best sign you could have, but he sure ain't out o' the woods yet.'

'What about them cows and that damn renegade Dixon?' Gilmore snarled before Wheeler could continue.

'I'm goin' after them,' Wheeler replied simply. 'Me and Travis and I figger one other'll be enough. Can't spare no more from the drive anyhow,' he finished simply.

'I'm coming with you, Cord,' Sammy snapped, before any one else could speak. 'Billy was my partner and I figger it's my right to square up for him.'

'Glad to have you, son,' Wheeler responded, a rare grin lighting his face. 'Cut us a coupla spare ponies out of the cavvy and . . . '

'I'm coming, too!' a cultured voice snarled and Wheeler turned to see an enraged Milt Gilmore jerking his saddle over his shoulder.

'All right, Mr Gilmore,' Wheeler agreed softly. 'Get your stuff. We're leavin', pronto.'

★   ★   ★

'Now what in hell d'you figger that could be, Cord?' Sammy Miller offered, pointing ahead to where a group of black specks circled effortlessly on the early day's steadily rising thermals.

'Don't know,' Wheeler responded, urging his big bay mustang into a distance-eating lope. 'But whatever it is, there's something still alive under them buzzards, 'cause none of them look like they're ready to set down yet.'

And so it proved.

Turning a shallow bend in the trail that they were following, Wheeler, pulling up abruptly, came upon the body of a horse.

'Brand's Flying F,' Sammy offered, reining in beside the man from El Paso.

'And it looks like one of Dixon's string.'

Before anything further could be done, a figure appeared from the group of rocks which bordered the trail and began to walk unsteadily towards the group of horsemen.

With a curse, Gilmore reached down and jerked free his borrowed Winchester because the figure walking towards them was none other than the treacherous foreman of the Flying F.

★ ★ ★

'So what you're saying is that you took off after the herd when you see Robles and his boys was aimin' to lift them?' Wheeler summarized blandly, after Dixon had told his story.

'But how come you took a shot at me, Wade?' Sammy demanded.

'I didn't, you bonehead,' Dixon sneered. 'I was shootin' over your head at one o' them fellas headin' off into the darkness. Don't think I'd have missed you at that range, do you?'

14

'So what in hell happened back there?' Gilmore hissed as he moved back next to Dixon early the next day.

'Why didn't you and that goddamn moron wait until we could get the whole herd?' the lawyer continued. 'Or better, do what you were told and hold that old fool Faulkener up for the coin when the cows were sold?'

The Flying F foreman had taken up a position in the back of the group as soon as they left the campground and Wheeler had been content to let him stay there, hoping that if Dixon felt he was unsuspected he might make a move that would betray him.

'Robles double-crossed both of us,' Dixon explained softly, turning so that no one in front could see him conversing with the lawyer.

'I figgered to wait and snatch the

dollars like you said, Boss,' he went on ingratiatingly, 'but when Robles's boys hit the herd and killed young Billy, well hell, I figgered best thing to do was trail along with them, pretend like I was in with 'em.'

'But it weren't no good,' Dixon went on quickly, apparently ignoring the other's snort of disbelief.

'Robles waited 'til we was down trail aways and then slugged me from behind — ' Dixon's words seemed to die abruptly in his throat because he suddenly found himself looking down the bore of a small pistol clasped in Gilmore's rock-steady fist.

'You expect me to swallow that?' the lawyer hissed. 'If he slugged you from behind, how'd your horse get shot?

'No,' Gilmore snarled. 'I think you and Robles were running out on me and figgered to split the herd money between you!'

'N-n-no, honest to God, Boss,' Dixon almost sobbed. 'He double-crossed me as well! I just want a chance to get even . . .'

For a long second the Flying F foreman's life hung in the balance, the lust to kill gleaming in Gilmore's deepset eyes.

'All right,' the lawyer hissed finally, slipping away his pistol almost reluctantly. 'You live . . . for now.

'How many men has Robles got?' Gilmore snapped after a moment's thought.

'A dozen, mebbe fifteen,' Dixon responded instantly. 'Too many for the two of us and what are we gonna do about that nosy detective? I ain't sure he swallowed any part of my story.'

'I've thought of that,' the other sneered. 'Are Robles and the scum that ride with him still camped in that hut on Little Mesa?'

Dixon nodded, too afraid to speak.

'Good,' Gilmore went on. 'Now listen carefully, you damn fool. This is what we're going to do and God alone help you if you make a hash of it this time . . . '

★ ★ ★

'Plain trail, Cord,' Travis Bregan offered as his companion swung easily into the saddle.

'Sure,' Wheeler said thoughtfully, staring ahead at the broad swathe of hoofprints that marked the passage of the remainder of the Flying F herd. 'Mebbe a l'il mite too plain,' the man from El Paso added. 'You keep the boys here. I'm goin' up to take a look. And keep your eye on that rattler Gilmore,' he ordered as he swung aboard his mount.

'Why more than usual, Cord?' Travis asked curiously.

' 'Cause I think it was the flash from his camera that started them steers runnin' back at the crossing. And I think he done it deliberate,' the man from El Paso explained.

'That's why you brought him along!' Travis ejaculated.

'Just watch the bastard. And be careful! *Adios*,' Wheeler finished, swinging his pony up the trail.

184

Obediently, Travis turned away, only to stop, his foot still in the stirrup, as a thin little melody drifted towards him over the faint breeze. Someone, somewhere, was whistling 'Shenandoah'.

★　★　★

On the face of it, the spacious cabin with its ramshackle attendant buildings and biggish horse corral seemed peaceful enough as Cord Wheeler inspected them in the light of the westering sun, later that afternoon.

The detective had managed to gain a vantage point overlooking the flat area of rock, barely two hundred yards square, on which the buildings stood, with what looked like a sheer drop a bare fifty yards from the main house.

With characteristic patience he settled down to wait, counting off Robles's gang as they moved listlessly about the place.

'Eleven ponies,' Wheeler muttered to himself. 'Three men in the barn, along with that jug. Two down by the corral.

Five. So where in hell are the rest? And who's watching the herd?'

As if in answer to his question, a group of four men suddenly exited the cabin and going to the corral, caught, saddled and mounted their ponies before sending the animals hurtling up the trail, which Wheeler had previously marked leading away into the mountains, approximately opposite the one which he had followed in locating the hideout.

Patiently, Wheeler settled down to wait once again.

Some thirty minutes later, a second dust-covered group came into sight dropping down the trail to the corral.

Leaving their lathered mounts to fend for themselves the newcomers headed for the barn where, from the sudden increase in noisy hilarity, they were clearly intent upon making rapid inroads into the contents of the jug the other three had been sampling.

Silently Wheeler shifted backwards and down the steepish slope, at the bottom of which he had left the bay. Collecting the reins, he swung aboard and turned the big horse back the way they had come, almost instantly finding a narrow track which led up and back towards the bandit's hideout.

* * *

It was growing dark as Wheeler left the narrow track he had been following and turned back into the mountains, heading roughly in the direction he had seen taken by the first group of men leaving the bandit's hideout.

Full dark had come and Wheeler had almost decided to camp and continue his search in the morning, when his nose caught a faint odour of cow while at the same time he heard the characteristic blowing of contented steers settling down to sleep. With a satisfied grin, he turned his pony upwind.

'Couldn't have been better if the good Lord made it on purpose,' Wheeler told himself as he looked down on the little basin of rocky ground now containing the contented herd, almost invisible in the darkness and, nearer to him, the faint glow of the herders' fire.

'Two men ride herd,' Wheeler muttered to himself, 'and them two that ain't herdin' camp across the only way in so's nobody can sneak the herd out from under them.'

Reluctantly deciding that turning the two sleeping outlaw's horses loose would only alert the men to the fact of the herd's discovery, Wheeler slipped away and made his way back to where he had hidden his own mount. As he gathered the reins to mount, a boot scuffed in the silence

'Don' bother to mount up, gringo,' a voice hissed out of the darkness. 'Just bring that nice pony this way.'

'You better tell us where your friends are, gringo,' the big Mexican who had captured Wheeler intoned, balancing a broad-bladed fighting knife in his hand, 'or pretty soon you gonna wish you had.'

His captor had conducted Wheeler to the camp by the trail which the detective had been watching only minutes before. He had roused his companion and the pair had tied Wheeler to a heavy log that they dragged into the camp, securing both his hands and feet.

'I am not a patient man, *señor*,' the outlaw went on, speaking reasonable but heavily accented English. 'Where are your *compadres*?'

'If I tell you,' Wheeler whined, thinking furiously, 'd'you promise to let me go? I ain't done nothin' to you or your friends! You gotta let me go!' he finished, allowing his voice to rise to a hysterical scream. 'You got to!'

'OK, OK,' the Mexican responded softly. 'You got my word. As soon as we find your *compañeros*, I send you off.'

'Get the horses, Miguel and the others,' he went on, in Border Spanish. 'We don' wanna keep this hero waitin'.'

★ ★ ★

'They're up ahead,' Wheeler whispered shakily, swinging down from his mount and sensing that his four companions had done the same. 'In that clearing. Now let me go like you promised.'

'No, *amigo*, not jus' yet. You got one more leetle thing to do. Jus' go ahead and tell whoever is on guard it's OK. We be right behind you,' his captor assured him.

Cautiously, Wheeler led the way around the little clearing and began to approach the fire.

'*Quien es?*' suddenly rang out from the darkness and relief flooded Wheeler as he recognized the voice of Travis Bregan.

'It's me, Wheeler,' he called, then instantly dropped flat and rolled to one side as Bregan's Winchester began to pour fire into Wheeler's captors as fast as its owner could work the action.

The three leading bandidos died almost instantly, caught in Bregan's merciless hail of bullets, but the fourth man, perhaps more suspicious than the rest, had been a little behind the group and managed to avoid the ambush, darting aside to drop into sparse undergrowth in an attempt to circle back to the horses.

Rising shakily, the man suddenly found his hair grasped in a sinewy hand as he was jerked off his feet and a razor-sharp point pricked his throat just above the throbbing artery.

'Keep very still, *amigo*,' said a voice icy as death, in faultless Border Spanish. 'Very still and you may live just a little longer.'

★   ★   ★

'You figger he's tellin' the truth, Cord?' Bregan asked sceptically, after Wheeler had given a brief account of his adventures and then questioned the prisoner.

'He's only confirmin' what I saw for myself,' Wheeler shrugged as Sammy joined the group round the fire after tying their unwelcome guest securely.

'Countin' these four,' Wheeler went on, 'that leaves eleven. Say two to one. That's long odds, so here's what I figger we do . . . '

★ ★ ★

'Don't forget, Sammy,' Wheeler cautioned as he left the youngster overlooking the cabin and prepared to slip down to the horse corral. 'Plug anyone who comes out of the cabin. And make sure you get 'em good. There's too many for us to take chances with. *Adios.*'

And with that final warning, Wheeler slipped silently down the slope, angling away from the single unlighted window of the main cabin as he did so.

Reaching the bottom of the scree and boulder-covered slope, Wheeler looked up, checking the positions his companions should be occupying. Seeing nothing, he gave a grunt of satisfaction before moving on. He might not have been quite so sanguine if he had been able to see Wade Dixon, because as Wheeler began his final approach to the corral, intent upon releasing the gang's ponies, Dixon was behind the main cabin, carefully scuffing together a pile of inflammable trash.

With a satisfactory pile accumulated, Dixon stood back and heart in mouth, the Flying F foreman thumbed a match alight and dropped it into the mass of kindling.

The tinder-dry material ignited with a dull roar and Dixon hurried back to his post, intent upon carrying out the second part of Gilmore's plan.

Wheeler had barely gained the corner of the corral nearest the cabin when he heard the crackle of the flames and the yells of the awakened bandits.

Almost instantly, the cabin door was jerked inwards and Wheeler found himself bathed in the fire's glow and a potential target for every man struggling and pushing to exit the building.

Jerking up his pistol, the man from El Paso emptied the Smith and Wesson into the mass of bodies in the door, throwing himself to one side into the dubious cover offered by the shadows in the big corral as the outlaws' bullets pecked the dust in his vicinity.

Desperately, he shoved cartridges into the pistol, jerking the weapon up in time to put a bullet into the first man who had managed to fight his way clear of the door. Bullets tore splinters from the post inches from his face and Wheeler rolled away towards the welcoming darkness, rising just in time to drive his last bullet into the first of a pair of figures which loomed menacingly above him.

15

Before Wheeler could make a move to save himself the second man was on him.

The rank odour of day's-old sweat and whiskey filled his nostrils as his attacker grappled him around the chest, pinning his arms and all but crushing his ribs.

'I'm gonna enjoy this, Fancy Pants,' Wheeler heard Robles's voice grating in his ear as the detective struggled desperately to free himself from the bear-like grip.

'I'm really gonna enjoy this,' the bandit leered, as he forced Wheeler step by step, nearer and nearer the precipice which formed the fourth side of the little plateau the buildings occupied.

Barely a yard from the edge, Robles lumbered to a halt. Feeling the pressure on his ribs increasing, Wheeler began to struggle afresh, butting at the big man's face and trying to drive a knee between his legs. But it was all to no avail.

Remorselessly, the pressure increased until Wheeler was sure his bones must break, when suddenly, over Robles's shoulder, Wade Dixon's sneering face appeared.

Without hesitation, Dixon lifted his pistol and drove a bullet into Wheeler's opponent. Abruptly, the pressure on Wheeler's ribs ceased and he slumped down to find himself covered by the gross body of his dead assailant.

Only for a moment, however, because Robles's corpse was almost instantly jerked to one side and Wheeler found himself looking into the yawning bore of a Colt, with Wade Dixon's eyes blazing above it.

Surreptitiously, Wheeler ran an experimental hand over his bruised and aching torsos drawing a deep breath as he did so. His ribs were badly bruised, not broken, but as Dixon moved round, so that Wheeler was between him and the cliff edge, the man from El Paso groaned theatrically.

'Water,' Wheeler croaked, bringing his legs up under him for what he knew might be the last desperate throw of the dice. 'For Christ's sake give me a drink o' water. That bastard's killed me.'

'You ain't gonna need water where you're goin',' Dixon sneered, clearly relishing the moment. 'I'm sure gonna enjoy this and I couldn't let ol' Lou have the pleasure o' finishin' you, Fancy Pants,' Dixon explained, consideringly.

'No, I wanted to do that all by myself. O' course,' the Flying F foreman went on, slowly easing back the hammer of his Colt, 'I can't take as long as I'd like over killin' you, you goddamn son of a bitch, 'cause your friends look like they've just about cleaned house, what with the fire an' all. But that don't mean you gotta die easy. Oh no,' Dixon whispered evilly, the cold sweat of anticipation breaking out on his forehead as he raised his pistol, 'that don't mean you gotta die easy . . . at . . . all.'

But in taking so long over his eager anticipation, Dixon had allowed his opponent time to recover and as Dixon lined his pistol, Cord Wheeler appeared to erupt.

One hand sent a scoop of sand into the Flying F man's face as Wheeler catapulted forward. But this time the man from El Paso's luck seemed to have run out, because even as he launched himself towards the blinded and almost helpless Dixon, the latter pulled the trigger of his weapon by reflex and the bullet caught Wheeler in the head just above the scalp, throwing him backwards and, with one unlucky roll, sending him over the edge of the cliff.

For a single brief moment, the detective's hand caught on the fragile rock lining the precipice, before this gave way and the hand, clutching its useless burden, disappeared over the edge.

It was several painful minutes before Dixon managed to clear his eyes of sand and when he had done so, he advanced carefully to the edge of the cliff, glaring blearily into the blackness below.

'Huh, cashed and good riddance,' the Flying F foreman told himself as he felt his way back from the edge of the cliff before rising and going in search of a canteen to deal with his stinging eyes.

★   ★   ★

When Dixon gleefully informed his esteemed boss, however, Gilmore wasn't quite so confident in his employee's abilities.

'You saw the body, then?' Gilmore demanded shortly as he watched Travis Bregan scouring the rustlers' hideout for a sign of his friend in the early morning light.

'Hell, nobody could live after a fall like that,' Dixon whined. 'He's coyote bait at the bottom o' them cliffs sure, Boss.'

'You'll forgive my pointing out that your record against Mr Wheeler hasn't been marked with sparkling success so far,' his companion reminded him acidly. 'I shall want clearer proof that Mr Wheeler is no longer with us before I proceed any further with my part of our . . . partnership.'

Leaving the disgruntled and inwardly fuming Dixon, Gilmore made his way towards the cabin where Bregan was sitting disconsolately on the packing case which had served the rustlers for a front step.

Secretly, Gilmore was satisfied that Wheeler would no longer trouble them, having examined from a safe distance the area of cliff Dixon claimed the detective had fallen over. For once the fool was right. No one was coming back from a fall like that, but his professed doubts should serve to bring the other to heel, even without the information Gilmore possessed, which would hang Dixon under his real name.

Hiding his smile, Gilmore came to a

halt in front of Bregan.

'Any sign of the esteemed Mr Wheeler?' he demanded brutally.

'No.' Travis shook his head disconsolately. 'I can't figger it. Cord wouldn't just run out on us.'

'Pah,' Gilmore sneered. 'These gunmen are all alike. Everyone of them will turn tail and run when the going gets tough.'

'You're a liar,' Bregan said evenly, coming to his feet to stand with his hand hanging loosely over the greasy, battered holster with its oiled Colt.

'Easy to insult a man without a gun,' Gilmore sneered, raising his hands from his side.

'Sure,' Bregan admitted easily but he didn't relax as he went on. 'So you better shut your mouth about Cord or start wearin' one.'

'Sammy,' Bregan bellowed, turning away dismissively and contemptuously offering the lawyer his back. 'We better get them steers movin' afore the rest o' them fellas come back.'

And so it was, nearly a fortnight later, that Maddy Faulkener, sitting on the top bar of one of the Videlio cattle company's shipping corrals was the first to see a faint plume of dust thrown up by the hoofs of a thousand steers driven up the trail from Cartuna by four grim-faced, hollow-eyed men.

'And you never found out what happened to Cord?' Charlie Faulkener demanded after Travis Bregan had finished his story.

'Nope,' Bregan admitted, a dusty arm around a wet-eyed Maddy Faulkener's waist. 'Searched the whole shebang. Just can't figger it,' he admitted, as a newly bathed Milt Gilmore strutted into Faulkener's hotel room, to pull up short at the sight of his erstwhile fiancé and her beau.

'I'm sure you're grateful to this gentleman,' Gilmore interrupted, coming forward and attempting to jerk Bregan's arm from its place. 'But I don't want my fiancé huddling up to some other . . . man.'

'Travis!' Maddy Faulkener snapped, as the irate young man leapt to his feet. 'I can handle this.'

'I'm breaking our engagement, Mr Gilmore,' she began. 'It's plain to me that I was mistaken about my feelings for you.'

'B-b-but,' Gilmore began, honestly taken aback, for once, that this unsophisticated cowgirl should reject him, especially in favour of one who in his much-vaunted sophistication Gilmore regarded as little better than an animal.

'You mean you're choosing this . . . this . . . br — person over me?' the attorney went on, awkwardly changing his choice of words at the last minute, Bregan's thumb having hooked itself into his gunbelt in close proximity to the butt of his Colt.

'I don't think I had much to say about it really,' Maddy informed the enraged attorney with a disarming grin in Bregan's direction. 'But I guess that's about right.'

★ ★ ★

'Hell, Boss,' Dixon offered reasonably when an incandescent Gilmore had tracked him to the hotel bar and informed him of the setback. 'It needn't make much difference. 'Course, you won't have the gal,' he went on maliciously. 'But then you wasn't plannin' to keep her around long anyhow, were you?'

'They still got to take the money back to Cartuna, ain't they,' the foreman demanded. Receiving a surly nod in confirmation, he went on softly, 'So it's sweet. No reason why we shouldn't trail along, is there? Especially if her fiancé and her brother have a little 'accident'. And it sure wouldn't hurt for Miz Maddy to have to find someone else to turn to, not havin' her brother or that damn 'breed around,' he finished insinuatingly.

204

For a long moment Gilmore regarded this man whom he had always thought of as his 'thing', muscle with little brain.

'I may have misjudged you, eh . . . Wade,' he began at length, tone mild and conciliatory. 'You've got brains,' the attorney complimented. 'Arrange your 'accident'. But don't fail,' he went on with some of his old asperity. 'Or . . . '

'Or what?' Dixon snapped.

'Or we'll have to think of another plan,' the other responded smoothly.

★ ★ ★

'How's about 'nother l'il drin', Travis, ol' buddy, ol' pal?' Charlie Faulkener demanded, staring owlishly into the bottom of his glass, before upending it mournfully on the greasy bar of Videlio's biggest saloon.

'You've had enough,' Travis informed him, pushing back the glass and bottle and shouldering his friend away from the bar.

In truth, Bregan was worried. They had begun their evening's entertainment in no very raucous style but the liquor seemed to have affected Faulkener out of all proportion to his consumption.

With Faulkener an unsteady awkward burden Bregan pushed through the batwings and out into the street, while in the saloon a lean brown-faced man in the garb of a Mexican *vaquero* looked calculatingly after them.

'Wha' we doin' here, Travis, ol' buddy, ol' pal?' Faulkener demanded loudly, as Bregan paused in the middle of the street, shifting his burden and looking round in the hope of seeing a friendly face.

No face materialized, however, and with a mild curse, Bregan resettled his burden and began to guide Faulkener's uncooperative limbs in the direction of their hotel.

Unfortunately, the saloon they had selected for their celebration was in the poorer, Mexican part of town and as

Travis staggered up the main street under his all but comatose burden, there was a sibilant hiss behind him and two figures, heads enveloped in the universal sombrero, stepped into the street, effectively blocking his way.

'*Buenos noches, amigo*,' the taller of the two leered. 'It is a very nice night for a walk, no? But a little dangerous if you don' know your way aroun', eh.' His companion burst into hysterical laughter and Bregan sensed rather than saw the two who had moved up behind him.

'Get on with it, Juanito,' said a voice in rough Border Spanish over Bregan's left shoulder, as the young man eased the all but unconscious Faulkener to the ground. 'Always you have to talk too much.'

Bregan was under no illusions. He had met this type of Border trash before and he knew unless he was either very lucky or very quick, this dirty street was where he would die. Someone else would end up marrying his Maddy and, with that thought, his resolve hardened. If he died, he'd have plenty of damn company.

'But Pablo,' the tall one who had spoken first went on, dropping a hand to his belt as he did so, 'a man must have convers — '

He never finished, because Bregan, continuing to drop to his knee after lowering Faulkener, swept out his Colt and drove a bullet squarely into the man's sneering face.

Without waiting to see the result of his shot, Bregan rolled to one side, scrabbling to his knees and triggering his second shot point-blank into the chest of the second man, who was a bare pace from him.

But it did no good. As he cocked the heavy weapon, Bregan saw what must have been one of the men behind him standing only yards away and lining a revolver in his direction.

16

The crack of a shot sounded even as Bregan was desperately trying to raise his pistol and, involuntarily, he shut his eyes and braced for the smashing impact of the heavy slug.

But it never came and when Bregan's eyes flickered open an instant later, he found his former assailant lying on his face, the unfired pistol a yard from his hand.

Moving carefully, Bregan kicked the pistol aside, before he noticed what must have been the fourth man lying in a pool of dark liquid near the shadow of an adjacent building.

With a careless foot, Travis flipped his former attacker on to his back and what he saw nearly caused him to abruptly lose his evening meal.

Dressed in a greasy mockery of hildalgo finery, the man was plainly a bandido of the lowest type. He had been shot cleanly through the back of the head with a powerful, large-calibre weapon which had split his forehead like an over-ripe melon and deposited most of his brains in the street.

Intent upon his attacker and keeping his stomach under control, Bregan suddenly jerked erect, his Apache-sharp ears catching the faint echo of a familiar sound.

For an instant hope flared, before the young man rejected it with a tightening of the lips. Whatever had to be done now was up to them. Dead men didn't walk.

★ ★ ★

'What about the fourth one, Travis?' a white-faced Maddy Faulkener interjected practically, when Bregan had brought his account of the night's proceedings to an abrupt end without, however, mentioning the sound he had heard.

'Fourth one?' the young man answered vaguely.

'Yes,' Dale Faulkener snapped weakly from the depths of his comfortable armchair, where he had been irritably esconsced for the last three days. 'The fourth one. The last man, the one behind you.'

'Not countin' those who are up against you is a bad habit, young man,' the old invalid went on, crustily. 'And it ain't one I'd expect an Apache to fall into!'

'You're right, sir,' Travis responded with a rueful grin, apparently ignoring Maddy's hiss of displeasure. 'But I was kinda busy at the time!'

Somewhat mollified, the old man smiled tightly and settled back in his chair.

'That fourth feller was curious,' Travis resumed. 'His throat had been cut but it was neater'n I'd ever seen it done before.'

'Just a l'il nick,' he continued clinically, smiling an apology at the girl as he

211

did so. 'Mebbe an inch long and right over the artery. Then through into the throat.'

'Neat as you please,' Bregan finished admiringly. '*Hombre* would've been dead in about fifteen seconds, without makin' a sound.'

'What sort of a knife you think would do that, Trav?' Charlie Faulkener asked blearily, having surfaced during the last part of Bregan's exposition.

'An assassin's weapon,' the elder Faulkener offered shrewdly.

'I don't care what it was, Charlie,' Maddy Faulkener said crisply, ignoring her father.

'We better get Dad to bed and then we all need to get some sleep. Don't forget you told the boys sunup tomorrow.'

It was sometime later as the two young men settled down in the bedroom they shared off the main suite, that Faulkener asked, 'What you figger about that knife, Travis? Ever seen one like it before?'

'Yeah, once,' the other replied thought-fully and with that, the young rancher had to be content.

* * *

'What's ol' Breck doin' here?' Travis asked mildly next morning, as he and Charlie Faulkener rode towards the stockyard's big horse corral, where the ponies of the Flying F's remuda had spent the preceding evening eating their heads off.

'What with Dad bein' laid up I figgered another man couldn't hurt,' Faulkener stated.

'Breck's a good cowhand,' he went on defensively. 'And he's sure a changed man since Sol got caught in that stampede.'

'Think you're right,' Travis agreed simply, kneeing his pony towards the big man where he sat his mount with Dixon, Sammy and Joe Baggs, the remaining Flying F hand.

'Glad to see you with us, Breck,' he

offered, riding up to the big cowhand and frankly shoving forward a hand. 'Need all the good men we can get on this trip.'

For a long second, the big man regarded the younger one, then, diffidently, he shook hands.

'Glad to be along,' he rumbled. 'Flying F's a good ranch and now we've put this drive through, she's sure due to get better yet.'

*   *   *

With the sun warming their backs and their bellies full the Flying F's remuda was inclined to be skittish and the crew had their hands full re-establishing the well-remembered drive routine.

By midday, however, the animals had settled into their old ways and Faulkener felt sufficiently happy with their progress to drop back to where Bregan was teasing his sister.

'You figger we mebbe ought to keep a lookout on our back trail, Trav?'

Faulkener interrupted worriedly. 'I'll sure feel happier when this' — he paused ostentatiously slapping a bulging pocket — 'is in the bank.'

'I'm way in front of you,' Bregan replied mildly. 'I been watching our backtrail pretty close since we left town. There ain't no one followin' us.'

⋆　⋆　⋆

The day passed uneventfully. Even old Dale Faulkener, more cheerful now with the smell of horse around him and the sun on his face, seemed amazingly stronger that evening than he had at the beginning of the trip.

Remarking on this to Bregan at the end of that first longish day, Maddy Faulkener received a shrug and a tired smile.

'It's hard for him,' Bregan said, before adding insightfully, 'And it's due to get harder. He's all right now, ridin' up there on the wagon, in the middle o' things. But have you thought what it's gonna be like for him when he gets home, seein' Charlie runnin' the ranch, givin' the orders he oughta be givin'? Hell, Maddy, he can't even fork a horse to blow off a l'il steam. I wonder what the hell that ol' man's thinkin?' he finished. 'He must be goin' through Purgatory.'

All thought of Dale Faulkener's predicament was driven from Bregan's mind, however, when at three o'clock the following morning, he was awakened by a boot driven unceremoniously into his ribs.

'Get up, 'breed,' a familiar voice snarled as Bregan, forcing his eyes open, found himself staring into the sneering features of Milt Gilmore.

Looking past the Cartuna attorney, he saw Charlie Faulkener, his sister and the rest of the crew, including Breck Barker, lined up in front of the chuck wagon and covered by the Colts of a grinning Wade Dixon.

Even Dale Faulkener had been dragged out of his blankets and propped unceremoniously against the rear wheel of the vehicle.

Without warning, Bregan received another kick.

'Get over with the rest of your friends, you 'breed bastard,' Gilmore snarled, gesturing significantly with the small-calibre pistol grasped in his right hand.

Unwillingly, Bregan struggled to his feet, stumbling awkwardly towards Gilmore as he did so. But the Cartuna attorney wasn't to be caught off guard quite so easily. He twisted swiftly to one side and slashed his pistol across Bregan's cheek, the foresight of the little Smith and Wesson inflicting a shallow gash.

'Now get over there, Indian,' Gilmore sneered, gesturing again.

'Why in hell are you doin' this?' Bregan demanded, as he complied with the order.

''Cause he's a goddamn, two-faced mangy coyote who musta been left on his father's doorstep . . . ' Faulkener began, giving full vent to his spleen.

Finally, running out of breath and invention the indomitable old man faced the evil-visaged Gilmore and his grinning henchman.

'So what are you two coyotes going to do with us? Come on, speak up, you coward,' Faulkener snarled. 'You needn't worry, Milt,' he went on, old voice hard and level. 'I can't get up and, anyway, I see you ain't got a quirt handy. Or do you just use that on kids?'

Stung beyond endurance, Gilmore leapt forward, slashing his empty left hand across the invalid's face.

'You coward,' Maddy Faulkener flared, instantly throwing herself between the two men and swinging an open-handed slap.

Too late to dodge, Gilmore was caught squarely, but with a lithe movement he captured the girl's arm, twisting it painfully up and behind her, while dextrously clapping the muzzle of his pistol against her forehead, freezing her brother and the Flying F hands into instant stillness.

'Now, Mr Faulkener,' Gilmore sneered, 'I'll be glad to tell you exactly what we're going to do to you.' He paused, relishing his power to hurt.

'We're just naturally gonna kill you, old man,' Dixon interrupted softly, the cold sweat-beads breaking out on his forehead. 'An' then we're gonna take your ranch!'

For a moment, Faulkener stared at his foreman open-mouthed before throwing back his head and emitting a bellow of laughter.

'What in hell d'you want that place for?' he demanded, when he had partially recovered. 'It's a good ranch, but it's nothin' special and it sure ain't worth the chances you fellers been takin'.'

'Isn't it?' Gilmore sneered, stung out of his usual self-control. 'How much would you guess your worthless piece of land would fetch, if I told you that the railroad intends to run a spur line from Videlio, through Snake pass to Cartuna and then on further south?'

'B-b-but, that'd make the Flying F worth, Christ, it might be millions,' Charlie Faulkener blurted. 'And even if you didn't want to sell they'd have to buy the right of way and with the line right on our land, Dad, why we . . . no . . . not just us . . . everybody'd be rich!'

'You won't never get away with it, Milt,' Bregan offered familiarly, hoping to push the attorney into a rash move. 'My pa and Uncle Joe'll catch you. An' if Pa let's Uncle Joe at you, an' he might if you hurt Maddy, you'll be a long time beggin' for death before it comes.'

Gilmore, however, had himself well in hand now.

'And why won't we get away with it, half-breed?' he sneered. 'There won't be nobody to contradict any story we tell.'

'We was attacked by bandits,' he began. 'And everybody but me and Dixon was killed, except Miz Maddy, who they captured, afore anyone could get to her. They'll have to believe that, especially when they find her body, a couple of miles from here, where the bandits left it after they had their fun with her . . . '

'That's the part I'm gonna really enjoy!' Dixon interrupted savagely. 'L'il Miz High and Mighty,' he went on, leering at the white-faced girl. 'Livin' up at the big house while the rest o' us cowhands work our asses off to pay for her fancy doodads. That goddamn white whore — '

'That's enough, you damn fool,' Gilmore snarled, cutting short the other's tirade.

'Here, take the girl,' he went on, motioning the other forward.

Swiftly holstering his left-side Colt, Dixon secured the girl and stepped back, without once losing the drop.

'Now who shall we dispose of first?' Gilmore freed from the encumbrance of the girl, mused as he flourished his pistol.

'Age before beauty, I suppose,' he went on thoughtfully, stooping to retrieve a pistol from the pile of weapons which Dixon had previously stripped from their owners, before coming to stand in front of a grim-faced Dale Faulkener.

'Ever see a man die of being gut-shot, old man?' Gilmore began with a sneer, then he jerked the weapon upwards, spinning on his heel away from the Flying F men because from out of the darkness there floated a thin, steel sharp sound.

Someone, somewhere, was whistling 'Shenandoah'.

17

'Now you and your l'il friend just drop them pistols before someone gets hurt,' a well remembered voice snapped from the shelter of the rocks rimming the camp site.

'That someone bein' you,' the voice added sardonically.

For a moment it looked as if the men concerned would comply, until Dixon suddenly jerked his arm up to encircle his captive's slim neck, jerking her backwards to shield his body before snapping two shots into the darkness.

But the erstwhile foreman of the Flying F had badly miscalculated the calibre of Maddy Faulkener.

As soon as the girl saw the muzzle of the pistol rise up in front of her, she wrenched Dixon's pinioning arm upwards and sank her strong white teeth into his wrist.

Surprised by the pain and acting on simple reflex, Dixon swung the girl away from him. Almost instantly, a Winchester cracked twice from the surrounding darkness and Dixon was thrown backwards to land in the dust, eyes unseeing and blood pumping from two bullet wounds in his chest, the holes close enough together to be covered by a single playing card.

'I ain't gonna tell you again,' Wheeler's voice knifed out of the darkness. 'Get rid o' that toy pistol, Gilmore, or you'll be ridin' to hell behind your friend.'

Slowly, Gilmore's hand opened and the little Smith and Wesson fell into the dust.

Instantly, Bregan darted forward, pushing the attorney roughly away from his weapon before lifting the little pistol, emptying out the cartridges and pushing it into his belt.

'Watch him close, *amigo*,' Charlie Faulkener offered, tossing Bregan his weapon-belt and drawing his own Colt in a continuation of the same movement as a familiar figure left the rock-bound shadows and walked into the firelight.

★ ★ ★

'Well,' Wheeler began, after the exclamations of amazement and handshakes were concluded. 'What you got to say for yourself, Mr Gilmore?'

'Why,' came the surprising answer, 'I have to offer you my sincerest thanks! Although why in hell you aren't dead I can't imagine.'

'Well, that's sure a new one on me,' Wheeler admitted softly. 'It ain't often I get thanked by a man who I'm gonna help to hang. Just why are you thankin' me?'

'Why, for saving me from the clutches of . . . that.' Gilmore responded smoothly, indicating the dead man.

'Dixon blackmailed me into helping him,' the attorney continued. 'I could do nothing. Now, his death has freed me. So, I have you to thank for it.'

'But you were givin' the orders,' Maddy Faulkener snapped. 'We all saw you.'

'That was how he planned it,' Gilmore whispered, passing a suddenly shaky hand across his face. 'My God,' he went on hoarsely, 'the things he threatened to . . . to . . . do to me if I didn't help him.'

'I — I'm not a brave man, Mr Wheeler,' the attorney whined pathetically, carefully watching the gun in Charlie Faulkener's hand. 'And when Dixon came to me, threatening me, why I . . . I . . . just had to agree. And it wasn't just me,' Gilmore finished brokenly. 'He said he'd hurt . . . Dad, too.

'I stood him out on one point, though,' Gilmore added almost as an afterthought. 'I wouldn't do his killing for him. Not that. Not whatever he threatened.'

For a moment, Gilmore thought it might just have worked. The three ranch-hands had begun to argue furiously amongst themselves; while Charlie, Bregan and Maddy were exchanging dubious looks, Faulkener, by now, having shoved his pistol back into its holster.

Then Gilmore's glance leapt back to Wheeler. One look at that cynical grin told Gilmore what his chances were more clearly than a million words.

'So what do you think, Mr Wheeler?' Gilmore began with what he hoped was a sincere smile. 'I hope you'll agree, I'm more sinned against than sinning,' he went on unctuously, moving inch by inch towards Maddy Faulkener.

'So you was just gonna ride off with him?' Dale Faulkener suddenly piped up, from his place by the wagon wheel. 'What, and hope he wouldn't just leave you somewhere out in those badlands?' the old rancher finished, struggling to lean forward.

'I — I really hadn't thought ... ' Gilmore began.

'No,' Wheeler interrupted caustically.

'That's been your trouble all along. Not thinkin'. You figger you're so smart and the rest of the world is so dumb, don't you, Gilmore?'

'But you've made mistake after mistake and left a trail a half-smart kid could follow,' the detective went on. 'First, you got no interest in socializin', town's folk are beneath a highfalutin' college boy like you. Then, within a coupla weeks of makin' out Dale Faulkener's will, you're sparkin' his daughter. Don't need no college eddication to figure that one out.'

'The best man you can find to help you is a hydrophobic killer.' Wheeler paused and indicated Dixon's body. 'Who's about as stable as a stick o' sweaty dynamite and has been on the rustle for years. And to cap it all you're a liar and you're no good at keepin' your lies straight.'

'Add to that, I found the body of John Sumner, the railroad surveyor you murdered, or leastways had murdered, up on the mesa and while I was waitin' for you to start from Videlio, I got a wire from Travis's pa. Seems the slug Doc took out of that greaser that got shot in the jail was a .32. Same calibre as that l'il pop gun Travis has . . . '

But while Wheeler was talking, Gilmore had been edging gradually closer to the group containing Maddy Faulkener and suddenly, with a single well-timed grab, he had plucked the girl towards him, at the same time sweeping his left hand under the lapel of his coat to withdraw it grasping the twin of the weapon now shoved in Travis Bregan's belt.

The men could do nothing but stand stock still as, with the light of near-madness flaring in his eyes, Gilmore backed out of the firelight.

Apparently satisfied with his position, Gilmore ground his pistol more deeply into the girl's side, drawing forth a gasp of pain. The sound seemed to inflame him.

'I want a horse,' he screamed hoarsely, tightening his grip on the girl.

'No wait, two horses, food and canteens as well. Can't leave my little hole card behind, can I?' he said menacingly; the little pistol bored in again.

'Or can I?' Gilmore finished voice low and threatening.

'Get the horses, Travis,' Wheeler finally ordered. 'And be careful with the saddle blankets,' he went on softly, keeping his voice low so that the Cartuna attorney couldn't hear. 'Make sure there ain't nothin in them that might . . . upset Mr Gilmore.'

'Sure, Cord,' Bregan agreed quickly, his face clearing as understanding dawned. 'I'll bring Jezebel, too!'

'And while we're waiting,' Gilmore ordered, leering past a half-strangled Maddy Faulkener. 'You better sidle over here, Faulkener, and ante up that herd money.'

'I ain't . . . ' Charlie began.

'One more lie'll be the last thing your sister hears!' Gilmore snapped, transferring the pistol to his right hand and driving the muzzle hard under the girl's chin. 'The money,' he went on darkly, stretching out a hand, 'or . . .'

With ill grace, Faulkener unstrapped the big thigh-pocket of his chaps and drew out the bundle carefully wrapped in a rough cotton bag that said 'Bank of Videlio'.

'Just throw it gently,' Gilmore ordered, before deftly catching and pocketing the bag.

'And I'll take the ponies, 'breed,' he went on, as Bregan led two saddled mounts into the firelight.

Wheeler's plan should have worked. But as Gilmore put his hand on the horn of the saddle having first motioned his captive to mount, the little pony whinnied and jerked back.

Realization dawned instantly and with a sneer in Wheeler's direction, the attorney snatched the reins of Maddy Faulkener's mount.

'I'll just take this one,' Gilmore ordered, dragging the girl from her seat and climbing clumsily into her place.

Unfortunately for Gilmore, Maddy

Faulkener's pony, Jezebel was a one-woman horse and the feel of a stranger on her back drove her to sun-fishing, buck-jumping madness.

Always a poor horseman, Gilmore could do nothing but hang on grimly as Maddy Faulkener instantly leapt back, leaving her enraged pony to deal with the killer.

Safely ensconced behind Bregan, she watched the final scene of the tragedy.

It wasn't long in coming. With a final enraged flick, Jezebel rid herself of her burden, Gilmore landing hard in the circle of firelight.

Unable to control the impetus of his landing, the man rolled once to end face down in the red hot coals of the camp fire.

For a single long moment there was silence, then it was broken by the fiendish shriek of a man in mortal agony.

In an instant, Wheeler had covered the distance between himself and the badly injured Gilmore but even as the detective reached down to drag him from the fire, Gilmore reared back, jerking up his pistol and firing in almost the same movement.

But Gilmore's aim was off and his bullet passed between the detective's legs, the wind of the slug brushing his jeans as Wheeler's foot lashed out, catching Gilmore solidly under the jaw and knocking him senseless into the dust.

'Shouldn't never try and help a rattler,' Wheeler reflected bitterly, shaking a rueful head at his own stupidity. 'You gotta either kill him or leave him alone.'

'Cord!' Travis Bregan was at his elbow just as Wheeler bent to retrieve Gilmore's little pistol and shove it into his belt. 'You better come quick! It's the old man. Gilmore shot him.'

One look was all Wheeler needed as he bent down beside the old rancher who had become a friend.

Striking high in the chest, the little .32 slug had torn its way through the old man's lung, leaving a bare few minutes of life. He rallied a little when he saw the face of the El Paso detective.

'Cord . . . ' Faulkener gasped, voice barely a whisper. 'How . . . how'd you make . . . '

'Back at the mesa?' Wheeler asked quickly, anxious to spare the old man. A feeble nod answered him.

'Hell, it weren't no trick,' Wheeler began edging round slightly so that he could see Gilmore, where he lay on the opposite side of the camp fire, scrabbling his way back to consciousness.

'I saw that cliff,' Bregan interrupted. ''Less'n you grew wings there weren't no way you coulda climbed outta there, even if the fall hadn't killed you, which it would have.'

'Sure,' Wheeler agreed easily. 'If I'd fallen down the cliff. Only I didn't.'

'Them cliffs was sandstone,' he went on. 'And they was full of holes, from l'il rat holes to full blown caves.'

'When I went over, I grabbed on to the edge. It didn't stop me, but it slowed me up just enough to bring me against the cliff. Only it wasn't cliff, it was one of them caves I told you about.'

'I ain't really sure how it happened,' Wheeler admitted, ''cause Dixon had managed to clip me with his last shot. When I more or less come to, everybody had gone and I was lying out of sight in this l'il hole in the rock.'

'Anyhow,' Wheeler continued, 'I climbed up the rock, which weren't no real job and had a look round. Oh and I lied to Gilmore. I never found that young feller's body. But I did find his suit and a letter from his ma in the cabin. Told me enough to know I'd guessed right about him being a railroad surveyor. Sure hope that boy died easy,' he finished grimly.

'Border filth . . . ' the elder Faulkener gritted painfully, 'ain't . . . '

'Yeah,' Wheeler responded. 'I know. It ain't likely. Anyhow, day or so after I got up that damn cliff, them rustler's ponies started coming back, for water I guess, so I roped me a couple and went after Travis and the boys.'

'Why'nt you join up with us?' Bregan demanded. 'We sure coulda used some help.'

'Nope,' Wheeler disagreed. 'You was doin' all right. And I was never too far away from you. Lucky I wasn't,' he added with a disarming grin, 'when them four greasers jumped you in Videlio!'

'I ain't arguing about that!' Bregan returned with an answering smile. 'But why didn't you let on you was alive?'

'Gilmore,' Wheeler began. 'I figgered to give him enough rope to . . .'

But the man from El Paso suddenly found himself interrupted by the rattling thunder of hoofs.

'Wheeler, goddamn your soul,' a hysterical voice screamed out of the darkness. 'I'll see you in hell!'

18

'Christ, it's that bastard Gilmore,' Charlie Faulkener bellowed, spinning on his heel and seeing the vacant spot where the attorney had been lying. 'He's taken the night horse!'

'Shame about the money,' Wheeler offered, watching a sanguine Travis Bregan as the others rushed to saddle ponies and pursue the fugitive.

'Money? What money'd that be, Cord?' Charlie Faulkener asked, pausing in tightening his cinch.

'Where'd you hide it?' Wheeler demanded, suspicions hardening into certainties.

'They put it in the flour barrel,' Maddy Faulkener interrupted. 'Charlie, leave that. It's Dad,' she went on, voice breaking. 'He's gone.'

★ ★ ★

'Let's get after that bastard,' Faulkener gritted, striking at his eyes as he turned away from the body of the old rancher, only to stop as a hard hand was laid on his arm.

'Why worry about that?' Wheeler said callously, jerking his head towards the hills. 'Doc Gilmore won't thank you for dragging him back and hanging's too easy a way for him to die.'

'No,' the detective finished. 'Let the desert have him. We gotta see to your pa.'

★　★　★

'So who was it killed them girls Cord?' Al Bregan demanded. 'Or are we still lookin' for him?'

The remains of the Flying F trail crew had been back at the ranch for a bare two weeks but already big changes were afoot.

None of them were of any concern to Wheeler, however, and he was now making his last visit to the Cartuna sheriff's office, before leaving for El Paso on the evening stage.

'No, we ain't,' Wheeler admitted, lounging back in the rickety office chair. 'I figure Dixon killed Millie Graham, for some reason I ain't sure about. I don't buy in to that story about him not being able to . . . well, anyhow, Gilmore musta found out about it and figgered that a story about some maniac killin' off blonde-haired girls would be useful if he needed to get rid of Miz Maddy, either before or after he married her.'

'So he killed the l'il Krantz girl and poor Miz Sadler just so's it looked like the killer was still workin'. Gilmore was clever about Miz Sadler, though, you got to give the bastard that,' Wheeler offered.

'I ain't follerin' you there, Cord,' Bregan admitted.

'It was Gilmore screamed when they'd dumped the body in the alley to make it look like she was killed there, I'm guessin', so you an' Joe wouldn't go lookin' anywhere else. Then, one of them faked the footprints so it looked like a big man had done it, which meant it couldn't be either of them.'

'And,' Wheeler went on after a short pause, 'I know why Miz Krantz wouldn't tell her pa about her beau.'

''Cause it was Gilmore an' he told her not to?' Joe Ironhand suggested, polishing his new glasses with a determined air.

'Yeah, that was my guess, but we was both wrong.' Wheeler grinned. 'She was sparkin' that Scots boy, works in the store. Being a Scot, he's a Catholic and . . . '

'Levi's hardline Protestant . . . ' Bregan finished.

'That's the whole story,' Wheeler shrugged.

'An' what put you on to Gilmore?' Ironhand demanded.

'He was too far out of place,' Wheeler said simply. 'Fancy Dan like him, somethin' was holdin' him here and it certainly wasn't his pa or his likin' for the town. That and his pa's hands.'

'Hank's hands nearly fitted the marks. Doc's got small hands for a man, some unusual in this town,' Wheeler explained. 'I guessed it might run in the family.'

'Then Joe found that reticule with some fresh splinters on it,' the detective resumed. 'Same as some I found on the door of Gilmore's darkroom, so Miz Sadler must have been there. And then I found that railroad surveyor feller's watch; Travis recognized it and told me that Gilmore knew him.'

'Gilmore wouldn't have nothing to do with a young feller like that 'less there was something in it for him.' Wheeler shrugged. 'I figgered a branch line, but the wire I sent to the company didn't get an answer, which I figgered was answer enough. God knows how Gilmore found out about the spur but he did and I got a feelin' it may have had somethin' to do with that fancy camera of his,' Wheeler said thoughtfully.

'You told me Gilmore had some trouble in a cathouse in 'Paso called Leonardo's,' Wheeler went on.

'Sure,' Bregan replied.

'Now, see, I know Leonardo's,' Wheeler admitted. 'And the speciality o' the house is blackmail. Mebbe that's where Gilmore got his hooks into young Mr Sumner.'

'Wouldn't be the first to run into that sort of trouble with the wrong sort of girl,' Ironhand offered.

'If it was a girl,' Wheeler replied gently, 'Leonardo's caters to all tastes and there were a coupla pictures in that jacket I found up on the mesa . . . '

'Anyhow,' Wheeler went on with a world-weary shrug, 'that's how it was. Gilmore probably blackmailed the story about the branch line through Snake Pass out of Sumner, then he buys up all the land on the other side of the pass, but to make a real killing he needed more time to get hold of Dale Faulkener's ranch. So he had Robles's men kill Sumner to delay the survey and set about gettin' the ranch.'

'Frightening how close he come, when you think on it,' Ironhand offered.

'What about Gilmore?' Bregan asked softly.

'Ain't sure,' Wheeler admitted. 'The pony he stole come back to the ranch about ten days ago, no saddle or fixin's. Wrangler said the animal was starvin' and thirsty but other than that, he was fine. It's any gent's guess what come o' Gilmore.'

'Hard way to go,' Bregan offered.

'He earned it!' Wheeler stated coldly. 'He never worried hisself about them gals or young Sumner when he let that Border trash have 'im. And what about when he started that stampede with his flashpowder and nearly drowned Maddy Faulkener? No, whatever happened to him, it weren't bad enough,' Wheeler finished vehemently.

'Talkin' o' Border trash, where did Robles fit in?' Bregan asked.

'I figger he was Dixon's man,' Wheeler shrugged, rising and picking up his bag, as the dust-covered stage pulled up with a massive creaking of harness in front of the saloon. 'They'd been swinging a wide loop for years and hadn't made the mistake of gettin' greedy. Anything else?' he finished mildly.

'Nope,' Bregan admitted, rising and shaking hands. 'Cord, I'm thankin' you. If you ever need anything, you let me know. And there ain't no limit on that, neither.'

'Goes for me too, Cord,' Ironhand confirmed, shaking hands in turn.

'That listens good,' Wheeler grinned. 'Can't have too many friends on the *right side* of the law.'

THE END

Other titles in the
Linford Western Library:

HARD RIDE TO LARGO

Jack Holt

When Jack Danner arrived in Haley Ridge he spent the night in jail. But then financier Spencer Bonnington offers him fifteen hundred dollars to escort Sarah, his niece, to her father's ranch in Largo. However, their journey is fraught with danger, especially when Bob Rand and his partners see Sarah as a prize and a means of ransom from the Bonningtons. Danner is being watched, but by whom? An easy fifteen hundred becomes the hardest money he's ever earned.

MOON RAIDERS

Skeeter Dodds

Wayne Creek is a family town, not overly prosperous. However, when Samuel Lane arrives with his own enrichment in mind, change is anticipated. Though the town might find affluence through him, it would also become dangerous, with the dregs of the West flooding in . . . Standing alone against Lane is Jeb Tierney. The scales of justice seem to be loaded against him — and yet nothing is quite as it seems. Will Lane, after all, get his much-deserved comeuppance?

THE SHERIFF OF RED ROCK

H. H. Cody

Jake Helsby figured there would be trouble as the rider headed into town. It had started when somebody put a piece of lead into Fred at his place, the Circle B. One of the hands reckoned the Grissom kid was responsible, but Jake was suspicious of the mayor's anxiety to hang the suspect, and of Lily Jeffords's interest in the kid's well-being. And even as he searched for the true culprit, Jake had his own dark secret to protect . . .

BAD MOON OVER DEVIL'S RIDGE

I. J. Parnham

Sheriff Cassidy Yates rides into Eagle Heights only to land in jail on an unfounded murder charge. Although Cassidy answers the charge, his wayward brother becomes implicated in the murder and the kidnapping of the dead man's widow. In a town gripped by a conspiracy of fear, Cassidy is helped by a newspaper correspondent to find the real killer and the kidnapped woman. But gun-toting ranchers and hired guns stand between Cassidy and justice — can he prove his brother's innocence?

THE RANGE SHOOTOUT

Carlton Youngblood

Buck Armstrong is looking after a company of paleontologists, searching for dinosaur bones on Ranger Big John Calhoun's land. But his problems are just beginning: after stumbling onto a bunch of rustlers, he's accused of being a rustler himself, and is kidnapped and left to die. Then, after he's saved by Cord, Calhoun's son, a stagecoach hold-up is blamed on Buck and Cord and the manhunt is on. Can Buck ever win through and discover what's going on?